Rebecca

John K. Sutherland.

April 2021

Robert was encouraged to take refuge on the upper floors of the Deming house when his friend, George, recognized that his mother was still, unexpectedly, at home, and was on the warpath.

That, was when he met Rebecca, George's sister, in the attic area of the house.

He had taken some time to see her with her sitting in a wing-back chair with her feet raised onto the window ledge in front of her, taking advantage of the sun.

She was sitting, carelessly, in the window space, facing the setting sun, with the last warm rays shining in upon her, bathing as much of her as was possible under her dress.

She did not seem to realise how exposed she was, what he could see reflected in the window, or how intent he was upon seeing more of her.

He was shocked to see her there, but he was captivated immediately.

She was avoiding her mother; succeeding, where George hadn't.

Robert would be stuck in her presence for quite some time.

He was stuck for long enough to fall in love with her, and to learn so much more about her, and about this peculiarly dysfunctional family.

Fate had directed his footsteps here.

Rebecca needed to be rescued, and he was the man to do it.

Contents

Another Step Forward.

A simple ceremony.

Noticing a Difference.

The next morning.

Learning to trust Rebecca's senses.

A difficult lesson learned. A house set in order.

A Chance Encounter. A House in Turmoil

As George Deming closed the heavy front door behind his military friend, Robert, he paused and listened to the sounds coming from deeper in the old house and echoing along its many corridors.

"Oh Lord! Mother's home, and she's on the warpath again." There was a raised voice from a not so distant part of the house.

"Thunder and tarnation! I thought she had gone off to her dressmaker and was still out."

He took in the time, displayed on the face of the Grandfather clock standing in the hallway.

"Damn! Can that be the time?" He dug out a pocket-watch from his waistcoat pocket and looked at it.

"Stopped! I suppose they will do that, when one does not wind them. No wonder she's home. I wish I had known that and we would have come in the other way. Quick, Robert, follow me upstairs. No, dear fellah, don't leave your hat or gloves here, and watch that you hit nothing with your stick; in fact, leave nothing for her to find.

"We will not be leaving by this door when we go out again, but another way altogether." His voice changed, to lend his next few words an air of theatrical mystery and secrecy. "We shall leave either by the sinister, secret passageway, or the craftily hidden stairs. I knew I should have gone onto the stage, instead of getting caught up in that damned theatre of war with Napoleon."

He made it all sound so eerily strange and melodramatic as he looked at his friend.

"Oh, the mysterious things that children discover that are unknown to their parents, though I did tell father, out of necessity. The less evidence of my having returned home, especially with someone else, the better, though as she checks my room regularly since I arrived back home from the Peninsula two weeks ago and is keeping track of my movements, it is hard to deny it.

"She wants me gone. Out of the house. I think she believes I may have brought one of those Portuguese beauties back with me, and must have secreted her somewhere about the house. Or some infectious disease. One could hide an army in this barracks of a place. But if she thinks I have brought some military friend home with me… then she will be sure to seek me out and whoever might be with me, and not let me hear the last of it for a devil's age, and she will be sure to insult you.

"She hates military men with a passion, including her only son I think, as well as any visits that she does not arrange for herself for a specific and limited time - and keeps away any visitors that are not of her own particular coven, or choosing."

George led the way up the stairs on tiptoe, making as little noise as possible as he gauged where his mother might be, from the distant sound of her voice. He spoke in a low voice so that only his friend might hear him.

"From the sounds of it, Robert, she is in the far dining room. Poor old Williams must have done something she didn't like. Perhaps he carelessly put a fish knife with the other knives, or did not arrange the glasses, just so, or there may even be a napkin with a minor crease in it, or a hair on the sideboard, even if it is one of her own. But then, she seems to bounce from one servant to another, and bounce, is the key word."

He led his friend along an upper corridor.

"If mother were the only one here for them to look after, they would all be long gone, and she would be forced to fend for herself, as she was for two weeks once, when everyone, including father and my sisters left to look after my father's ailing mother.

"She watches how far she goes with them, now. That was too much of a wake-up call for her. It is father that does the hiring and firing and not her. No-one would come to work for her once the word was out. I believe even the bats had cleared the attics by then, driven out by her shrill voice."

He paused and listened, to be sure where she was.

"I think they do it all deliberately now... do different things to annoy her... to keep her constantly frustrated, and permanently off balance, and out of Rebecca's path."

Robert did not ask who Rebecca was.

"They are very protective of Rebecca, and we are too. Rebecca is my younger sister, and seems to be the focus of much of mama's anger. If I could, I would see her taken out of here to live with our grandmother, but the old lady is not well, unfortunately, and cannot deal with my mother as she would like to."

Robert was happy to listen to his friend and not interrupt him. They would have plenty of time later, and had much to catch up, on in the meantime.

"Once up here and in the back part of the house we can be sure to avoid my mother. She dislikes it intensely when I bring a friend home, and I have no intention of inflicting her legendary moods upon you or anyone else if I can avoid it, nor upon myself either. She can be embarrassing and can all too easily put one to the blush in any company."

He paused again.

"If she is crossed, or obstructed in any way, she will fly into a screaming rage for as long as a week. Father takes himself off. I joined the military and went off for years, and my sisters keep their heads down and stay out of her way as much as they can. She can take a delightful day, as this turned out to be, as I did not expect to bump into you as I did, and she can turn it into one of the worst."

He relaxed more, the further he progressed into the rambling old structure.

"She rarely comes up here, except that she will go up the back stairs and check on whether I am home or not, so that she can ring another peal over me. My room is down there…" He pointed further along another dark corridor they were just passing. "She will find something to rake me over the coals for, so I will get you to wait for me in another room on an upper floor, before we make our escape again! I just hope she does not find out that I am home." He sighed heavily.

"Home! Some home!" He paused. "We should wait here for a few moments until I hear her elsewhere. The floor creaks loudly, there," he pointed, "…and we can wait for her to relocate, or she will be up here in a flash thinking it is my next sister, and I will not inflict our mother upon her! She can't hear us however, if we talk quietly. She is deaf to most conversation she does not instigate or direct, or does not wish to overhear."

He turned and briefly checked his appearance in a mirror beside him. He brushed a small leaf fragment off his coat.

"When did you land?"

"Two days ago! We had a very fast trip on board *the Corinthian*. I was ordered to check into Greenwich first, to see my surgeon, and they gave me enough of a pass that I might leave. Too few beds anyway, and I did not wish to stay. I was walking wounded, so I walked. They decided not to do any more digging. They have now washed their hands of me. I had long ago decided to cash out, the moment I set foot ashore. I was just leaving my tailor when I bumped into you, or you into me."

"So, we are now both free of the military. I almost regret it, considering what I have come home to. I had forgotten how much I hoped that she might have changed with age, but she hasn't. No matter; my problems are not your problems. You had enough of your own to deal with. You don't seem any the worse for your injury. We were not sure you would survive on the battlefield, once that damned surgeon went at you."

"It wasn't so very bad."

His friend knew better than to believe him. Perkins was a good surgeon, but did not have the time to waste worrying about any pain that he might inflict. You always knew where Mr. Perkins was located once the action started, by the screams that came from the operating tent.

"I survived Perkins, didn't I? He did manage to get most of that metal out of me, so I can thank him for that, and he didn't take any legs or arms off me, as he usually did! But what of you, after we got separated in that last action?"

"I survived it, much to my surprise. I never saw so much metal flying about. I managed to avoid your fate."

He held up.

"But later, dear fellah. She's moved again. We can go now, but stay to the right. The floor makes less noise over there."

They bypassed the noisy section of flooring with minimal disturbance, and moved deeper into the darker regions of the house, and then up another flight of stairs, on to a much darker, and higher floor.

"She won't come up here too readily, even if she hears the floor creaking now that it is getting toward dusk. Or I should say, especially not if she hears it creaking. The old family ghost!" He paused and put his hand on his friend's arm.

"You can go into the last room on the left down there and wait for me, Robert. There should be a book or two or a newspaper there. Father and I like to escape occasionally for a moment of quiet discussion without fear of interruption. She is loath to go to the upper floor when it is getting gloomy outside."

He looked furtively about.

"I should not be even half an hour, though if she gets to me first, I might be longer, so do not get impatient. I'll send one of the servant's up if I am likely to get stuck, and he will see you out. Help yourself to the wine but go easy on it. You're not out of the woods yet, my friend, though you've packed on a few pounds since I last saw you when you were all skin and bone in the field hospital, and not expected to pull through."

He watched as his friend proceeded along the corridor to the end and let himself in to that far room, then he turned and retraced his steps downstairs to go to his own room.

An interesting Conversation

Robert opened the door that George had indicated, and was surprised at how large the room actually was.

Everything was relatively dark, except for the embrasure over by the window where the heavy curtains had been pulled aside, and a window opened. The curtains were gently moving in the breeze coming in through it.

The fading rays of sunlight, penetrating almost half-way into the room, were clouded with fine dust from the floor, stirred up by the freshening evening breeze. The cooing of pigeons, settling for the evening, came from a ledge somewhere just outside of the window.

He was surprised to see that the room was almost entirely unfurnished, with no carpet to cover the rough boards; no pictures hanging on the walls, but one of them, the wall opposite the door, sloped too steeply for that. The other, next to the corridor from which he had entered, was vertical and very high, but still contained no hangings of any kind. There were two dining chairs by the wall next to the corridor, but no cupboards or other furniture except over in the window space. There, he could see that there were two wing chairs in that space, along with a small table between them.

His friend had been right about the books and magazines however. They were carefully and neatly arranged upon the table, along with what appeared to be an unopened bottle of wine and two glasses. It would be a pleasant room to escape to, if conditions downstairs were as his friend had described, and he had no doubt that they were, from what he had overheard. He had no desire to meet Mrs. Deming other than to put a face onto a shrill voice, and read of her character what he might.

He was known to be a good judge of character, and had a reputation of being unerringly able to select men of the highest caliber to serve under him. But where one might be able to read a man quite well, he had no success being able to gauge the character or mood of a woman, and was not fool enough to try.

Mrs. Deming sounded to be the worst kind of scold. In an earlier time, she would have been put into the stocks, or in the ducking stool.

At times like this, encountering unhappiness and turmoil where it should not exist, he began to commiserate with his friend.

Fortunately, his own mother had not been anything like that. She had been a kind woman, devoted to both her husband, until he died some two years earlier, and her only son. But with the loss of her husband from a severe infection, and the news from the Peninsula that her son had been grievously wounded and was not expected to live, she had lost the desire to linger on, herself, and had joined her husband within six months.

The reports had been wrong about her son's impending death. He had survived that war, and his injuries, and had gone on to become distinguished, and well-mentioned in despatches. He had been loath to return home at that stage, having lost both his father and then his mother, and with nothing to return to except an empty house and memories. He'd kept the servants on, and had allowed the house to be leased out while he was absent, as it was in a desirable location, as was this one, with its large grounds and rambling style, from an earlier age.

He walked over to the window, picked up a magazine from the small table, and sat himself where the fading light from the window might allow him to read for at least a few minutes.

He was startled to hear a voice beside him.

"You are not my brother, nor my father, so I think I do not know you, sir.'

His mouth almost dropped in surprise to notice a young lady sitting to one side of him in the other chair, which had been turned to face the window. She had been motionless, and partially hidden by the wing sides of the chair, and was sitting full in the bright light from the setting sun that had almost blinded him.

She was obviously amused by his sudden surprise – he may have drawn his breath sharply. He thought he detected that she smiled, though she still did not look directly at him.

"I heard you come in downstairs with my brother, and then followed your progress in your successful efforts to escape Mama. That squeaky floor is usually everyone's undoing if they forget it. Everyone tries to escape her, but they do not often succeed."

He chuckled gently with mild surprise and disbelief that he might have so easily missed someone sitting so close. But how had she heard them come in? They had been very quiet. He looked at her profile as she stared out of the window into the garden below, paying little attention to him, though the smile still lingered.

He apologized. "I am sorry. I did not know anyone might be in here. You startled me for a moment. George did not warn me that anyone else could be in here before me. Please forgive me, my name is Robert Hannan."

She seemed to have no shyness. "Hello, Robert Hannan."

Her face turned briefly toward him. She seemed to have her eyes closed against the bright light of the sun on her face.

"I am Rebecca Deming, the eldest of the Deming daughters, and two years younger than George."

That made her twenty-one years old. "I often come here at this time of evening to enjoy the last of the sun. It is so pleasant to listen to the birds getting themselves settled for the night; to hear the wind through the leaves, and catch the occasional noises from the far-off streets, and even from the river when the wind is right. The smell of flowers from the garden, especially from the lilies, is fading too as the season advances again, unfortunately.

"I do not like Winter so very much, and the sounds of insects - apart from that fly trapped inside - are also dying down. It is pleasant however, to feel the last of the sun's warmth, and a cool breeze upon one's face. Toward noon, this room can become stiflingly hot in the sun, being up under the roof as we are, even with the curtains closed. I prefer them open at this time of night, to let everything cool down."

As his eyes adjusted better to the room, he noticed better, the sloping, closed-in rafters, that extended from high overhead, and down to within about two feet of the floor where they met up with the vertical walls of the lower part of the house.

She sat forward in the chair, close by the window, attentive to everything going on outside, with her legs brought up in front of her. Her chin rested on her knees in that position, her arms resting on her knees, with her feet splayed on the edge of the seat.

He was not sure what might hold her attention outside and turned a little to see what he might see. Her reflection in the window, showed that with the sun full upon her, she was now clearly illuminated beneath her dress, sitting as carelessly as she was. Perhaps she found the warmth of the sun to be pleasurable upon her bare skin, but she was not aware that he might also see her in that way, sitting where he was.

The revealing vision of her unclad lower body, reflected in the window, and even a little magnified by a flaw in the glass, was interesting to him, of course, as well as exciting to see in all of its entrancing and intriguing detail.

He was powerless to look away. If he had been a bird, sitting on the window ledge outside, she could not have been much more exposed in all of her delicate, feminine detail, to his view.

He realized that she was unaware that she was captured by the glass acting as a mirror, almost directly in front of her, and beside the one section of window that was open.

It turned an innocent relaxing moment for her, into one of disturbing exposure for someone else sitting in just the right place, as he was. It began to disturb him too. He should not be attentive to her the way she was, but he could not help himself. He turned his head away before she might see what he was staring at.

He noticed that she was without shoes, with her bare feet poking out from the bottom of her dress and over the edge of the seat, yet there were no shoes on the floor below her chair.

She did not seem in any way concerned that she was alone with a gentleman she had never met before.

"I am sure that it will soon be too dark for you to read easily. Do you have something to open that wine bottle with, please? I would not mind a taste of wine at this moment, and we can toast the setting sun, and pray that the roosters will wake him in the morning again."

He was relieved to note that she had been unaware of what had been innocently revealed, and what he had just as innocently seen in rapt admiration.

"I am sure I can find something that will do the trick, Miss Deming."

He produced a small sheath knife from his belt and worked gently at the cork until it released with some additional prying from his fingers, and was pulled out with a gentle, 'plop'.

He poured a little of the wine into one of the glasses. It was a clear ruby red and had a good aroma. He passed it across to her.

"No, you can put it on the edge of the table please, where I can reach it, and I will get it in a moment or two."

That entrancing vision under the edge of her dress, was still there.

He put the glass within her reach, as tore his eyes away again, deciding to leave the bottle uncorked, to breathe for a few minutes. He watched as she unwound herself slowly and carefully from the chair, closing off that other tormenting view from his eyes.

She was obviously aware that he was watching her so closely. She reached out to the edge of the table for the glass, still focused on something happening outside of the open window. She retrieved it without upsetting it, as he feared she might, and took a gentle sip of it.

She sighed in delight.

"Not so very strong after all! You may top it up please, if you will." She looked over to him and held it steady as he poured. "You should join me sir. I do not like to drink alone, and I think you may be waiting some time for George. Mother has now discovered him, as he feared she might, and she is reading the riot act to him. He will not escape quite as readily as he had expected without having her fly into a towering rage, and no-one wants that, so he will put up with her until she lets him go. I hope you did not make any serious plans for this evening."

George would not be returning.

He had not heard anything from the floor below. She must have exceptional hearing, but then the recent noise of guns had robbed him of catching those gentle sounds that he had enjoyed as a youth, though he could hear the birds beginning to settle. "No, Miss Deming, I no longer have serious plans at any time of night or day. I am still finding my feet in the city, and am thankful to be able to do what I can."

"Ah. Recently returned from the wars!" She then startled him with an unexpected question. "I take it you were seriously wounded, or you would have been back much earlier. All of the other soldiers came back months ago."

"I was laid up for several months, but I am almost fully recovered now."

"I can smell the hospital about your clothing, yet you give no sign of suffering any serious loss of limb or crippling injury. "She paused. "Will you do something for me sir, please?"

"Yes. I will." He did not hesitate. He waited to hear what she might request of him.

"Please walk over to that far window and close it. There is a little too much of a breeze across this floor at the moment, and I fear it may take some of the papers off the table."

It had also undoubtedly been cool with the breeze blowing onto her exposed skin under her dress, as it had been. He put his glass down and walked as quietly as he could, over to the window at the opposite end of the large room and closed the window as she requested, before he returned to his chair.

"Thank you. That will limit the breeze, and it will also stop mama from coming upstairs. She seems to be wandering. Poor George."

"A creaking floor, and the family Ghost?"

"Exactly, sir." She laughed gently. "George told you of that. Unfortunately, she will now return to George before he has time to escape her and to join us."

He watched as she sipped at the wine, and he took in her clothing a little better than he had, though she was now better covered. He hoped she would not notice his stare. Her attention was still directed mostly out of the window, and with the little remaining light in her face, she would be unlikely to see where he was looking, seeing as much of her as he could without inviting her censure.

She had regular features, and a clear complexion. She was, in fact, beautiful. However, she had on a drab, and threadbare dress that had seen much better days, and it had a very large dark stain on the front of it. It looked like ink. The bottom hem was also showing signs of wear. Her hair, the most striking part of her after her features, was tidy, and well kept, and clearly received much attention, and in the last rays of the sun it shone almost bronze, as the light was reflected from it."

Why did she not dress, up to her social station?

"You are staring, Sir." He was embarrassed that she had caught him looking at her as intently as he had been. Could she have seen what he was looking at earlier? If so, she did not take him to task for it.

"I expect you are wondering why I am in my bare feet, and why I am wearing such a decrepit and time-worn dress that is so badly stained."

He had wondered.

"I am sorry! I should not have stared as I did, but I am naturally curious. I cannot help that. We know nothing of each other. It is certainly no business of mine how you choose to dress."

"No! But I will tell you. I am barefoot, partly from choice, as I do not wish to clump about the house and to wake everyone up. I keep late hours, as do we all, except for Mama. But the main reason is that when it gets dark outside, as it almost is now, and is somewhat cooler, I like to walk in the garden, and I prefer to be in my bare feet for that.

"In this house, we all lead three separate lives, children and servants both. Papa too.

"When Mama is in full voice, we all keep out of her way, and that, is one life. When she is not here, then we all do whatever it is we choose to do that we cannot easily do when she is here; that, is a second; and then at night, after Mama has retired out of fear of the wandering spirits; that, is when we are most free and can wander as we please, and do as we wish without fear of being spied upon or caught.

When it is dark, Mama cannot stop me, as she cannot see where I am, and she dare not go exploring alone without any light to comfort her. I wear this old and stained dress because I also like to poke around among the flower beds and tidy them a little, though she prefers, in any case - I should say that she insists - that I dress this way, to discourage me from going further afield outside."

It sounded like she was some kind of prisoner within the house.

"The last time I was allowed into the city was when father took me with him in the carriage, but that was a long time ago, and she was in a dreadful mood over that for almost a month. She had been terrified that someone might have seen us."

He digested what she had to say, not understanding what she was saying. There was much he would have liked to have asked, but stayed with the less obvious question.

"Why should your mother wish to hold you close to home? Why would she be afraid of you being seen? You are as beautiful as any lady I have ever seen. With a little more fashionable clothing, you would rival any of the beauties that grace any ballroom in the city. You speak well, and gently, even with a rough stranger such as myself."

"Oh my. You are flattering me unashamedly, Sir, and are making me blush, and you should not do that. You have also been in a ballroom? How interesting! I would like to hear of that, and of those other ladies; what they were wearing? How they did-up their hair? What jewelry they wore? Their shoes; what they spoke of? How they deported themselves?" She sighed.

"George believes that Mama is jealous of me, but she is also very afraid for herself in another way!" She could not look at him at that moment, with her attention almost fully outside of the window, but it was also too dark to read her expression. It seemed strange that there was no candle to be lit, and that they would sit in the dark, but she said nothing of it.

"You sound to be gentle and kind yourself, Sir. I did not detect any deception in your voice when you paid me such outrageous compliments as you did, so it is nice to know that you seem to believe them to be true. I think I heard George speak of you at least once, since he returned, and he spoke well of you then. But I do have much better dresses, which Mama does not know about, or she would remove them from me, or even...." Her voice tailed off.

"I wear those in the late evening when everyone else is abed. I like to be suitably dressed for entertaining, even though I do not entertain, and have never done so before, except it seems that at this present moment, I am entertaining you in my home, and have even been able to offer you a glass of wine. I am sorry if I seem to talk along without stopping. Once I get started I have difficulty holding back. I have so few friends that I can talk to, except for my sisters, and no-one apart from them, and my brother and father, ever visits me."

She was easy to listen to. She had a pleasant musical voice, much like the wind-chime he could just hear in the garden below the open window, and he did not mind that she rambled on. He would happily have had her talk to him all evening, without uttering a single word himself. He had not been able to relax like this for too many years.

Even in unfurnished and strange surroundings it was strangely pleasurable. She was both pleasant to look at, though difficult now in the darker room, and even more pleasant to listen to.

"Usually, one of my sisters would be with me, but they have been sent off by Mama, for a few days, for some reason known only to her, but it cannot be good, so I shall endeavor to stay out of her way. I also fear I will be unable to get to the garden as I would like. It rained the last two evenings, and if I am discovered leaving the house in the usual way, through the house, especially in daylight, then I will suffer for it and be locked away again. At least she will try, but there are no locks in this house that do not have many keys, and I have most of them, hidden in those same rooms. The other way, may also be closed off to me after a rain. I need help to open the way, after that, once the wood swells."

He did not entirely understand why she might be locked away. It seemed that her mother may be one of those few who hated her children.

"Could I help you there, perhaps?"

She turned her head toward him in the dim light, but he could see nothing in her expression to judge how she might receive that offer.

She considered for a few seconds and made up her mind.

"You have a gentle voice, and express yourself as someone I might trust. I do not see why not. And you are well known to my brother. You and George will need to leave in the same way, but George will not be likely to appear any time soon, so I will need to show you, so that you can make your own escape. He must have warned you about staying away from the rest of the house while Mama is on the loose, but if he didn't, then I will. I shall also show you the way over the garden wall. It is a light scramble to the top and then down the tree on the other side. The only difficulty might be in my getting back up here, if I go with you down to the garden."

"I could see to that too!" He watched her turn the last drop from her glass onto the floor as a gift to some unknown God, or little-known saint, presumably, and heard her glass as she put it onto the table after draining it.

"Then come! We shall go down a secret way known to all of us, but not to Mama, or she would have them all nailed shut."

He saw her vague outline as she stood, and then she reached over, touching his sleeve and took his hand, which in itself was quite unexpected and surprising. She seemed not to mind touching him, even with a slight familiarity. Her hand was very warm and soft to his touch.

"I will need to lead the way, now that it is quite dark, or you will blunder about and perhaps bruise yourself, as well as alert the house, but I will also need a little more strength from you, than I can use, to open the way up from up here, and again when we are down below too, and into the garden."

A hidden Way.

Rebecca led him across the room, and he followed her instructions to kneel down by the wall. He felt her guide his hand onto the wall, just a few inches off the floor.

"You will need to press quite hard there, to trip the latch and to move that part of it back, and to open up the stairway."

He pushed. Nothing happened. "You will need to push harder. If you can." She paused. "Oh! Perhaps you cannot. Your wound."

"My wound is not stopping me."

He pushed harder, feeling the latch, trip.

She pushed at the wood, swinging that part of it open, into the cavity behind.

"It's open."

She explained what lay ahead of him, but he could see that it was only a small opening, leading into a very dark place.

"There is a hole there, very dark, and it is about four feet down before you come to a small landing. You can see nothing without a light, so I shall need to instruct you. You will need to go in, feet-first, and then I will follow you as you turn to help me."

She could see difficulties for herself following him, in her dress. But recollected that it was dark, and he would not be able to see her clearly, if at all.

"I will then get you to help me to stand with you, and then we will go from there. I hope you are not shy! Do not move too much in any direction, or you will go down the central well, or the stairs, head over heels, and they are very hard and very steep, and you will certainly injure yourself."

She felt him slide through the hole to reach his footing, and then she sat down and put her feet through to follow him as she sat on the floor, and moved herself forward over the edge. Her dress slid up her legs as she did that, with it snagging on small projections on the rough floor.

"You will need to hold me, sir."

He pulled her dress to cover her better, and reached out to hold her at the waist to help her, wondering how she could be so relaxed about this, and with him touching her so familiarly after just meeting each other.

When she felt him holding her at the waist, as she instructed, she turned to lie on her front, to avoid bumping her head, and felt him easing her legs through the small space with him to join him in the narrow and confined space. And it was very confined.

She turned to face him with difficulty, brushing up, close to him. There was not much room, and he was stooped over, having discovered that the roof was close above him.

"We will need to change places, Sir, so that I may be out of your way, while you close this entrance, but do not close it entirely. Leave a small gap to get it open again."

He felt her pulling him close into her as she maneuvered around him. It would not pay to be shy, the way she held him, afraid that he would lose his balance.

She was not shy, or even slightly embarrassed, and did not shrink from being close to him despite knowing nothing about him. He sensed that she might even be smiling. He was. She was entirely unexpected and one surprise after another.

"George found this way out of the house years ago when he was endeavoring to escape, Mama. She believes that the attic room is a roost for bats, and she is terrified of them, so we play on that fear and others that she has. Nothing much would persuade her to come up here. The perfect escape."

She was amazing, and so innocently charming. As her hair brushed against his face, he caught a faint scent, but he could not put a name to the fragrance. Following her instructions again, he bent his head out of the way, as she held onto him, and by feel alone, he helped her push the piece of wainscoting back on its hinges, and almost into place."

"Damn!"

"What is it? What is the matter, Robert, Mr. Hannan."

He liked the way she had so easily used his first name.

"I have left my hat, gloves, and stick in that room, leaning up against the window."

She gurgled. "It does not matter. Leave them! You can come back and get them later and we shall find out if George managed to escape, Mama. I think I will need your help to return anyway after the rains."

They slowly changed places again.

"You must listen carefully, Sir, before we move to go anywhere."

He was listening. He preferred it when she'd called him, Robert. But she had easily used his name once, so would probably do so again.

She did. "You must listen carefully, Robert." He was certainly listening, holding her at her waist as she returned her hands to rest upon his arms.

This unexpected closeness, was very moving for him.

"There is a steep drop to your right. We shall change places again, and then you shall go first, down the stairs, while I give you instructions."

He felt her hair against his face again, and her body up against his, feeling her pushing against him, holding him close to her without any concern, or hesitation, or shyness, as they changed places once more.

He was careful how he moved, and where he placed his foot, cognizant that she was without shoes. He didn't want to step on her toes, and was concerned that she might get splinters in her feet, except the wood felt smooth and even slippery from frequent use.

She paused for a moment, listening to sounds from the rest of the house, but probably hearing only his heartbeat, and then she gave him instructions to get him safely down the narrow stairs in the pitch black, telling him what to watch for, and where he could hold onto.

He wanted just to hold onto her, keeping her safe, having just found her, but he would have to rely upon her instead.

"There are six steps down to another landing, where we will pause, and then there is a turn to the right in the stairs."

He counted the steps down to the landing, being careful not to hit his head against numerous sharp edges in the narrow space, as she kept a hand on his shoulder, following him closely, warning him to watch that he didn't hit his head, or he would likely draw blood.

He was careful.

There were enough handholds at the side and in front of him, as he descended the steep stairs—she was able to guide his hands to some of them—that once you knew the structure of the stairs and could picture it in one's head, they were easily enough traversed to the bottom. It was entirely black now, even blacker than before, if that were possible, as though they were standing in the bottom of a well, but she came close against him once more, holding onto him as he held onto her.

She seemed to have no shyness with him at all.

All he could hear, was her breathing and speaking softly to him, giving instructions, warning him where there were more projections to avoid. He was even more conscious now of her being very close to him, even in his arms, as he was, in hers.

Had there been a candle, there would have been none of this difficulty, but there had not been a candle, and he felt somehow glad of that, liking the feeling of her being very close to him all of the time.

She would be able to smell 'hospital' on his clothing again, but without her suffering the memory of what that smell meant to him; fading hope, pain, hours of uncertainty, then slow recovery for the lucky ones.

He had never had such a vibrant, relaxed young woman so close to him before, close enough to feel too much of each other, or with them so careless of social conventions upon such an early meeting, and without them being properly introduced.

He could feel her breath upon his face as he had turned on those landings to help her down to stand with him, and she would also be able to feel his breath upon her. What was she thinking of this circumstance?

He should not have drunk so much of that wine, but that was not all that was making him unsteady.

No. He should not hold her too close, as he was tempted to do, or to kiss her, as he so felt like doing. She would feel betrayed, push him away, and he would feel destroyed.

George should have warned him about her! He should have introduced them.

It was easy to put his arms around her as they stood there, and as she gave him further instructions about where they were and how they would move from here.

Without her, he would have been helpless. With her, he was almost helpless too. He was helpless to ignore her, and everything about her where they were. The darkness seemed to magnify all other senses and sensations.

He spoke her name, without realizing that he had spoken it aloud. "Rebecca."

"Yes. That is my name, Robert. We should be able to use each other's names, considering where we are and how we are helping each other."

She sensed him swaying, and held his arms more securely.

"Be careful that you do not bump your head or overbalance from vertigo in this blackness. There are many awkward places here."

She led the way now, with his hand upon her shoulder, half upon her dress, and half upon her warm neck, driving him even more breathless and mad.

"Almost there, just a few paces along here now, Robert. I hope you do not mind me using your first name… and it is all on the flat."

He could say nothing. He just wanted to sit down with her, where they were, bring her into his arms, and go to sleep.

"There is a latch on the wall just about head-height for you, directly in front of you. You will need to pull it down, and that, will release the mechanism."

He felt her turn to face him, leaning into him, felt her hand take his and guide it in the black of their narrow dungeon up between their bodies... brushing gently against... his mind refused to function for a moment at what he'd felt... and then onto a small projection there, just above her shoulder. Her hand was soft and warm. Everything about her was warm. He could feel it. He was also breathless.

Was he alive or dead? What was he doing here with this angel? How could she trust him? She must not trust him.

He heard her speak again, telling him what he must now do. All he wanted to do was to pull her to him and kiss her.

Focus. Focus.

It would have taken him ages to find that latch without her help, with him completely disoriented in the dark. He put his fingers over it and pulled, feeling a section of the wall start to move away from him, then they both stepped out into the cooler, moist air of the garden, away from that confining space. She preceded him, holding his hand.

It was still too dark to see very much, but he knew where she was, touching him the entire time. He heard her move the section of wall back into place and then she took his hand again and walked into the garden with him.

"Your eyes will soon adjust, Robert. It is a little lighter out here than upstairs, and there are few nights which are entirely black. I shall guide you again. I know every inch of this garden."

His nose was immediately assaulted by the scent of flowers, and he could now hear some of the fainter noises from the city and from a few of the surrounding houses, their windows lit by candlelight.

She did not let go of his hand.

He was in paradise! This, must be death.

In the Garden.

He felt her arm slide through his, as she led him across the lawn. He could hear, as she stirred her feet through the grass and then let go of him to twirl beside him with a gentle laugh, sending her dress flying. She was enjoying a few moments of freedom, but he could see little of her, though he could sense her excitement.

She took his hand again.

"If I can open the way for myself, I come down here most nights if the weather is fine, and spend hours out here, sometimes until it begins to get light. There is a small garden seat that I sit upon at the far end, and just listen to all of the sounds of evening and sometimes even, the insects during the day too.

"It is out of sight of the house, and Mama does not know that it is there. She never comes out here, as there is a beehive over there." She pointed.

"She hates fresh air, and sunshine, and she is terrified of being stung. We often mention how they will swarm, and attack even if they are not disturbed, but we mislead her, because they don't. It is so nice to be able to share this with someone else other than my sisters, though I do love their company, and they are so considerate of me."

He felt her take his arm again, not objecting in any way. Why would he? She was in a world of her own and was obviously happy.

"Come, we need to let James know that we are here. I am sure he heard that latch get released and knows that I am outside now."

She led him to one corner of the garden by the house, and spoke softly.

"James?"

A voice answered immediately from out of the darkness.

"I was not sure you would be able to get out without help, Miss, after those rains, with the wood being swollen."

"It was swollen, and hard to open, James, but I had help. This is George's friend – Robert Hannan – He is stranded for the moment, as

Mama has latched onto George, poor boy, and he will see that I get back in, safely, won't you, Robert?"

"Yes, Miss Deming, I will. "

"Are you one of the Hannans from Rutledge gardens way, Sir?"

It was strange to be questioned by someone Robert could not see in the stygian gloom, but then it seemed that they would not dare show any light, for fear of discovery. Mrs. Deming must be a formidable tyrant of a woman to put everyone in such a fear of discovery.

"Yes. I am. The last one."

"I know. I was sorry to hear about your parents. Your father was very well known to me. I served with him in the navy some years gone. When you have more time, Sir, and are in a different place, I would like to hear of your experiences abroad too. Your father did tell me a little of you when we encountered each other."

Robert felt Rebecca's arm tighten in his, as she pulled herself closer to him.

"How nice! You two know each other! In that case, as you know Mr. Hannan, James, perhaps you could persuade him to stay and dine with me. With Margaret and Helen gone for a few days, I do not like the thought of dining alone. He was promised to George, but it is obvious that Mama has other plans for my brother."

"I don't see why not, Miss. Your mother is out of the way roasting your brother, as you know, and if I use the dumb waiter in your room, I can have a meal up to the top there without much of a problem, and she would never know what was going on.

"George's pain shall be your gain! She heard that floor in the attic, creaking, a while ago, and I doubt anyone could pry her from her sitting room now, and she has no intention of letting George go just yet either."

"We will need a candle or two, as well, James. You should also be sure to secure my door to my bedroom, so that she cannot get into it to discover me gone, as I may not have time to let myself into it to change before we dine."

Yes, Miss, I know. I'll see to everything. You will have time. There will also be hot water waiting for you in your room."

Robert heard a door open, releasing a small streak of light from within and then it was closed off again.

"How exciting! I shall be dining with a gentleman other than my brother or my father. My father will not be back until very late, I expect. I hope you do not mind?"

Everything was running away from him far too quickly, leaving him confused and breathless.

"I do not mind at all, Miss Deming…"

"Rebecca. My name is Rebecca. You did so well there, for a while."

"Rebecca. Though I doubt your father would approve of you dining alone with a stranger such as I. I also need, and value the company…the change, and to dine with a beautiful and gentle young lady is always preferable to any alternative."

She digested his words for a few moments.

"I almost think I believe you. You sound sincere! My father would not object if it makes me happy. My mother would, object, but I don't ask her permission for anything.

"In any case, I am of age to make up my own mind what I shall do, and James will protect me if you turn out to be a thoroughly bad character, though I don't think you are."

"Then I must be on my best behavior, and try very hard, not to be the thoroughly bad character that I usually am. I am surprised George did not tell you more about me. Warn you. Others would tell you the same.

"However, you can believe me, when I told you that you are beautiful, as it is true. You are beautiful! I have been away from gentle society for five years, and I never missed anything so much in all of my life as a beautiful smile or the gracious presence of a woman. There was little beauty where I was, and few, gentle women. But yes, I am not too bad a character where young ladies are concerned, though I am a bad character with others when the need calls for it."

"George said something like that too, about you. You are not a total stranger. Then I shall cautiously believe you on both points! One needs to be deprived of some things to appreciate them better, I think.

"A man should also know himself well enough to be able to admit to his failings, as you just did. It makes you more believable. I think also, that, since we were destined to become friends, once George mentioned your name, and you will be dining with me tonight, that you will please call me Rebecca, all of the time, rather than forgetting, and calling me, Miss Deming. Let us not lose ground with each other."

"Rebecca, then, and thank you, and I am Robert, as you know. Now, where are you taking me?"

"I am taking you to the rose garden, Robert! That was the scent that almost drowned out all others while I was sitting in my window; that and the heady scent of the tiger lilies, though there was also lavender, and a smell of damp leaves, as well as the not entirely-unpleasant smell of the stables."

She stopped.

"Listen! The worms are out now and rustling through the leaves. It is going to rain again. And there is a fox somewhere quite far off. Did you hear it cry out?"

He had.

"You will need to bend down a little, and you must watch for the thorns." He felt her hand guiding his, once more in the dark, to touch a rose in full bloom.

"That, is a yellow one! It has a slightly different scent from this one," she guided his hand again, "… which is red."

He sniffed at them both, as she suggested, but could not detect any difference. Her senses had certainly not been dulled by loud noises or the burning stink of gunpowder.

She led him still farther afield, speaking almost never-endingly about the garden and its wonders, even addressing a remembered flower as if it were a person, or carrying on a conversation with the birds she knew were now roosting just overhead.

She knew, and explained everything to him in the large garden from one end to the other, before she let him sit with her upon the wooden seat up against the wall. It was a narrow seat and they were pushed close together, but he did not complain, even when her arm went around him to give them a little more room.

He felt her warm leg against his, and was conscious of her arm around him, and that she still held tightly onto his arm, leaning into him with her head against his shoulder.

This could not be happening to him. Her hair was against his cheek again. He would have liked to have turned into it and felt it upon his face, but dare not. He found it disturbing. Pleasantly, and alarmingly so.

"This, where we are sitting, Robert, is where you can get over the wall when you leave tonight if you do not leave the usual way, although I shall be sorry to see you go. First-found friends – alliteration – are the ones most difficult to part with, as you can never know when you will encounter them again.

"You stand upon the back of the seat to get to the wall top, and then there is a tree on the other side that you can climb down. This is how George, and even father at times, leaves or comes back into the house to avoid Mama when she is parading about in one of her infamous moods.

"I do wish she were not so unhappy. She either rages, or she cries. There is nothing, anyone can do for her no matter how hard we try, and we have tried.

"This part of the garden is invisible from the house, so no-one can see anything. I think I told you that already. And we cannot be overheard if we keep our voices down."

She took a deep breath.

"Robert?"

"Yes."

"If I were to ask you to do something for me… would you?"

What could she possibly ask?

"Yes. I will do anything you ask."

"Would you kiss me, please, Robert?"

She felt how that request startled him.

"Oh, dear. I am sorry. That is far too forward of me. A lady should not ask that. I should not have asked, should I?"

"Probably not." He felt that she had become agitated over requesting that.

"But, you see… I have never been kissed by a gentleman before, and none of my family counts. Oh, dear! Perhaps we should just go back in."

She would need his help to rise from that seat, but he was not ready for that.

"You say you have never been kissed before?"

"No, Sir." He sensed her blushing.

"Robert." He reminded her of their agreement about using names.

"Robert."

"Neither have I been kissed by anyone like you, Miss… Rebecca."

They both became silent.

"When we stand up to go in, if you would still like me to do that, to kiss you, then we can kiss each other."

She squeezed his hand, recovering quickly.

"Thank you. I would still like that."

Something else caught her attention.

"Oh, listen, Robert!" She leaned into him, resting her hand on his knee.

"That is Charlotte, the girl who lives in the next house along. She plays the harpsichord so well, and she has a beautiful voice to go with it. I sit out here often at this time of year and listen to her for hours. They know that I am usually out here just after dark. I have occasionally spoken to them over the adjoining wall between the two gardens. I used to play the harpsichord too, but Mama took it away from me."

They sat still and listened for some minutes; minutes that seemed to extend to perhaps an hour.

In truth, Robert would have been contented to have sat there all night, and to feel her close beside him, and as infectiously happy as she was.

She did not seem in the least bit shy.

"We must go back in now, Robert! It is getting chilly, and I need to bathe, and to change my dress so that I may not present too shabby an appearance for you to dine with.

"James must wonder where we are. He will serve us when we are settled."

They stood up together. He took her by the shoulders and turned her to face him, moved his hands to her face, leaned in and kissed her on the lips for just a few seconds. A lifetime. He'd never felt so confused in all of his life.

She said nothing, did not push him away, did not object.

They strolled back to where they needed to re-enter the house and climb up to that room again. They were holding hands now.

Robert was in love!

What are your intentions?

Robert followed her instructions for opening the downstairs entrance from the outside, closing it carefully behind them firmly, until he heard it latch, and they returned to the house the same way.

She went up the steep stairs ahead of him, leading the way as he touched her in the small of her back, with her having to let go of his hand on those steep stairs. Even in the dark, he was conscious of everything about her; her swishing dress as she climbed, her personal scent--vibrantly alarming; her breathing; the intoxicating way she affected him, leaving him breathless.

And she had even dared to ask him to kiss her!

He was still confused and recovering from that kiss. He also knew he should not be here. He was not safe for her. She was not safe for herself, encouraging him like that. He had not been close to a woman like her for many years. He had never been close to a woman like her!

Rebecca excused herself once he was settled in the window space again, and went to her own room in the far reaches of the house.

It was obvious that George would not be joining them.

Robert was left with his thoughts, as he finished off the wine he had left sitting in his glass, and began to think about this strange circumstance and this wondrously confident beauty that he had discovered.

He noticed then, that he had been able to see what he had of her when they'd returned, because a Candelabra had been placed upon the table, which had been cleared of all but the wine and the glasses, and the table had been set for two to dine.

James had been busy while they had still been in the garden. He may even have been able to hear them from up here!

An older man entered the room. This must be James. He had closed the window and drawn the curtains across so that no-one might know, once a candle had been lit, that anyone was up here.

Robert felt an unusually firm hand upon his shoulder, holding him in his seat, wincing at the sudden pain, but he said nothing.

"Now then young man. We need to talk, candid-like, and man to man!" It sounded... no-nonsense, serious of a sudden. Indeed the older man had a stern look upon his face as he looked down upon him.

"I need to know what your intentions are with Miss Deming, and I need an answer now!"

He saw hesitation and a slightly pale face as Robert looked up at him, meeting his eyes unwaveringly. He had caught the young man off guard.

Good!

"I hope you gave up those ways you had, afore you was sent away, for they was the talk of the town for a while. Oh, yes, I knowed about them! I didn't like what I heard, and I need to hear better from you now."

Roberts eyes still did not waver from his.

"I will tell you this. If I think you are gammoning me, or if you so much as harm a hair on that young lady's head, I will kill you, I will. It might be the end of me. I know all about you, and you a fire-eater, as well as a womanizer, but my life means nothing compared to hers."

He waited for a response.

"Got your tongue, did I? Daren't admit to anything?" He saw the young man smile up at him.

"Sir."

"Call me, James. That's my name, and we spoke earlier in the garden. I can tell you this, however; if you cannot satisfy me, here and now, that I have nothing to fear from you with regard to that young lady, whom I love like my own flesh and blood, you shall be out of this house in the twinkling of an eye, and I shall make suitable apologies for your absence, but go... you... will, no matter how excited she may be at her unexpected company."

Robert looked up at the old man towering over him. Determined! Even threatening! He could see that he meant what he said.

Robert spoke quietly.

"James." He took a deep breath and considered his words carefully before he spoke them.

"I honestly do not know what my feelings are at this moment. I am not sure I have any feelings left other than despair and anger." James knew better than to break into the young man's suddenly analyzed thoughts.

"I am recently returned from war, where I saw all but a few of my friends cut down beside me; while I lived. I buried them, and then buried even more after them, while I, managed to cheat death, on every occasion."

James saw the pain of recollection, cloud his thoughts.

"I was given up for dead more than once on the battlefield, and in the hospital, and yet I am still alive. I lost my mother, and my father, both needlessly, while I was away. For some inexplicable reason, I still live." He sounded as though he had difficulty believing that. "At least I think I still live. There are times when I doubt it." They were difficult memories.

"I used to weigh the best part of fourteen stone, and now I weigh barely twelve – some if it, metal that will never come out of me until after I am dead, though I did weigh only ten at one time, a couple of months ago.

"I am but a shadow of my former self at the moment, empty inside and out, yet I am almost as fit and as strong as I ever was in my body, if not in my mind. Almost.

"You ask a strange question that I am struggling to answer as I need to. You speak of 'feelings', but I am not sure that I might ever feel anything anymore." He paused and contradicted himself. "Though I now find that that is not true. I do have feelings. Strangely foreign feelings for me after all of that hatred and violence. So much blood spilled, and to what end?

"I think I would rather have died in the place of many a better man than I am. Then you, suddenly ask me of my feelings and of my intentions for that strangely wonderful young woman I just met, and who has more life, and promise in her gentle touch and soft words, than I think I might have left to me in my entire body."

She had achieved a wondrous transformation in him.

His voice caught and his eyes misted over.

"Whatever it was that you heard of me, or think you know, I cannot say. I have not been privy to those rumors.

"However, I know that I set society against me some years ago; most of it well deserved. But I also know that some of what was said, and believed of me was false, and was deliberately spread. I was never a threat to any woman, despite those tales. But I could not correct it. There were powerful men aligned against me, and I killed to protect myself, and my family from them." He sighed.

"I was not believed then, nor do I expect you to believe me now. What I cannot deny, is the violence I brought to bear against those who thought to kill me before ever I went abroad, when I fell afoul of the wrong people. That was true enough. I am no less violent, I am sure, since that time, perhaps more prone to violence when called for-- war does that to any man-- nor am any more inclined to walk away from those offering me violence, and there are one or two of those others still wanting to be revenged on me.

"Despite all of that, I can only repeat that... never... have I posed a threat to any young woman, and I do not pose one now! In truth, although I may have few of those more civilized and rational feelings of any kind, and need to learn them again, I think I begin to feel as you do even, having only been in her company for barely an hour…"

"Try, three hours!'

"That long?" He looked up disbelievingly at the older man.

"Aye, that long! You were in the garden for almost two!"

"I think, if I dare say it, on so little an acquaintance, and expect to be believed, though I don't…" he looked directly into the older man's eyes. "…that, as brief as our acquaintance has been; Miss Deming and I, that I would kill to protect her, just as you would.

"That is why I went abroad; to protect such as she from the greater ambitions of Napoleon. I do not understand it just yet, the why's, or the wherefore's of it, but that is the way it is!"

James's expression softened as he listened.

"I want to laugh with her, and at other times I feel like crying like a child. I find that I am a stranger to myself even. I swing from one mood to another without knowing why, and that, is as much to do with another life behind me now, as it is with this one, of a sudden. I am finding my feet again, gradually. And then I meet with one such as she, and understand once more what life can hold and even offer; if I dare think on it, or if I dare dream about a future I do not deserve with what I have done."

James was not about to interrupt.

"At the same time, I am afraid of what I might do. Not to her. But to defend her! I have seen too much injustice and horror, and unhappiness, and I did not expect to come back to see any suggestion of it here. I cannot understand it yet, but I find that I want to take her away from this, as wrong as that might sound, and so soon, although I am not sure what 'this', is, just yet, but I know that I do not like what I have heard or seen up to this moment. This is not a house at peace! I sense that she is not treated kindly, and that makes me... fearful of what I might do to correct that. She deserves much better than she knows at this time."

He shook his head. 'Those are my feelings at his moment."

James stepped back a pace, obviously moved by Robert's strongly voiced feelings and impressions.

"Thank you, Sir. Yet you have not seen the one hundredth part of it!"

He made up his mind about many things. "I shall tell you what 'this', is Robert. I do trust Miss Deming's instincts about most things, and possibly, even about you. I have not known her to be often wrong."

He took a deep breath.

"This house is, as you surmise, not at peace. It is a kind of purgatory; one before death rather than after it! The fiend that rules it is a woman. Her mother; no-one else, but she was not always like this."

His glance softened. "As for the other, about you; the violence... the women! I heard they was lies too; the one about the women, and from a very good source, and not from your father when he lived. I'll find out better, and more, very soon."

He smiled at him.

"Well, quite a strange surprise you have turned out to be. I think you will be staying for dinner after all."

Robert had not expected to be allowed to stay after what he had said.

"I did not expect any such kind of an answer, but I like it for the moment. I heard your regiment had been through one hell, after another, as though singled out for destruction. Listening to you, I can see that you spoke true. Sometimes, the lucky ones were them as didn't come back.

"She will be with you soon. Afterward, you know how to leave... down that other way and over the wall. Do not go or come any other way unless you are told otherwise.

"Take this with you." He placed a length of ribbon in Robert's hand. "If you come again – and you will – I can see it in your face, heard it in her voice in the garden, and saw it on her face too, when she passed by me on her way to get changed, in her excitement; tie this around that thin branch that extends out and touches the house window, and I will know you are here, anytime of day or night. I can see it well-enough against the lights in the other house, and I shall find you. When you leave, see that it goes with you. Do not lose it."

"I won't."

"God help you if you have misled me, but I don't believe you did. Now, I shall surprise you again. Where might I find you, if the need is there? Are you in your father's house?"

Why would he want to find him?

"Yes, I am."

"If I ask you to come to help her, will you? Though I know that is a strange request, knowing so little of any of us, and on such brief acquaintance."

Robert did not hesitate in his answer.

"I think I would walk through the portals of hell to protect her, though my fire-eating days are over for the moment. I am but a shadow of my former self!"

"Good! You are still more than enough for most men from what I saw of you. You may have to walk through those portals, but I think you will manage well enough. The inner man is intact, if the outer is not there yet. You will soon regain your full strength. Her brother will not be tolerated here much longer after tonight! They both need to see him gone, mother and Rebecca, both, but for different reasons. Her father too, and then she will try to do what she has intended to do for many years, though we shall block her. It is coming to that time when a more decisive action may be needed to deal with her mother. This madness is not who she really is."

James was lost in his own thoughts for a moment.

"Rebecca's grandmother, Lady Deming, is helpless in all of this. She is too old and too infirm, but will move to intervene if the need is there. She will be an ally. She cannot do much at the moment, as she does not wish to make things harder for her son than they already are. He still loves that woman he married, as I still do... despite... and is loath to do what may be needed, but that time is coming.

"One more thing, Sir. "His voice dropped so that he could barely be heard.

"When you leave this room, extinguish all candles, even if she is still here. I shall see everything is cleared away before morning. I am always somewhere close. She does not need them to get about in this house.

"I sense that you may not know this, but Miss Deming has been blind for many years now, but you should not say anything to her about it.

"Her mother is afraid that others may discover this too. She is driven almost mad, regarding it as a terrible affliction upon the entire family because of something she did to cause it, and it is tearing her apart from inside. Her mother can now barely look upon her or can be in her company without her malice towards her becoming obvious. She is a very stupid woman to reject the most prized of her possessions if she did but know it. However, she wasn't always that way.

"There you have it then."

The old man left without saying another word.

Robert sat there for some moments, strangely upset by what he had just heard about Rebecca's affliction, yet so much was explained now, in her open manner and accidentally intimate behavior by that recognition.

It all began to make sense to him. She might not 'see', in the usual way, but her other senses more than made up for it, and with a sensitivity that defied his understanding, until now.

He also learned something else that had gradually crept over him in that last hour, or two, or three, since she had first spoken to him. He was in love for the first time in his life, and it had nothing to do with feeling sorry for her apparent predicament. It had happened before he even knew of that, but had everything to do with him, and how she had affected him, as he had listened, and conversed with her!

He looked about himself as the weak candlelight illuminated the far reaches of the room.

He began to wonder if he were not in a dream of some kind, and yet suddenly his life began to seem as though it might have a purpose to it after all. Perhaps he had been allowed to live for a reason, and she was about to join him, so that they could dine together and get to know each other.

Dining Together. And then….

Rebecca re-joined him no more than five minutes later. She breezed into the room as gracefully as any gazelle, dressed just as well as any duchess, and curtsied toward where she knew he must be, watching her.

She had hurried her ablutions just for him.

She presented a far different appearance than she had, earlier. Her hair was the same, but it was now tied back with a strip of ribbon, the same color ribbon as that in his pocket. Now, she had on a blue dress with ribbons sewn onto it, and she even had slippers on her feet, just seen beneath the bottom of it. He found he could not take his eyes off her, yet she saw none of his shocked surprise, though she knew he would be watching for her, and knew where his eyes were directed.

He stood, moved a dining room chair out from the table, making just enough noise that she knew where he was, and was waiting for her. She approached the table as he took her arm and brought her into the chair as he moved it under the table as she sat down.

He sat opposite her.

"You are looking very charming Miss Deming, Rebecca. A notable change."

As James waited upon them from time to time, they dined together and talked at length. He could not remember all that they spoke of.

From time to time, James appeared and cleared the dishes away and brought others. He noticed that Robert had an appetite that would soon see him put back his weight that he had lost.

None of it was lost on Rebecca, who saw everything, while seeing nothing; analyzed every word, every intonation, and every nuance of the way things were said.

After their late meal, they moved across to the wing chairs and sat facing each other, closer now, as she had made sure the chairs were pushed closer, barely six inches apart, though slightly offset to leave room for their legs beside the opposite chair, so that she might touch his arm as she spoke, and to gain another measure of him.

There were moments when she unconsciously took his hand in one or even both of hers, as they talked. She seemed to be able to see him. She did not have that look of a blind person, where they just gazed unblinkingly, able to see nothing.

After a moment of silence, she asked very quietly; "Robert? Would you object if I were to touch your face, and discover more about you?"

Although taken aback by her words, he found that he could not refuse her such a simple request but was not sure what to expect. He realized that it was but one way she might find out much more about him; as, having lost one sense, she would bring others into play to make up for it.

He readily agreed, not sure what to expect or how it would be accomplished, and was surprised to find that she left her own chair and sat on the arm of his, and very close to him, as she placed his hand from that chair arm, across her legs as she sat there.

She placed her hands first upon his shoulders and slowly and gradually felt his upper arms, and then came back to his neck. She said nothing, pausing often.

He had missed a few hairs under his chin when he had shaved that morning, and she noticed those too. She may have found that strange.

With her hands on each side of his head at first, she slowly and lightly moved across his ears... his hair, unruly and even wiry... and then traced out his eyebrows, also thick and wiry. She paused and then went over some of it again, returning to his forehead, on, to his cheeks, nose, and lips, and all so carefully done.

His arm rested nervously across her warm legs, with his hand at her hip as she sat close into him. She dwelt longer, and moved more slowly over his lips and his eyes than anywhere else; seeming to concentrate her entire attention on what she was doing, and learning about him.

She went over his face again, as though to find what she could have missed in her first exploration, and to make a map of all of his features in her mind.

He resisted the urge to move forward into her hands, though she would undoubtedly be able to feel his warm breath upon her palms, and that his rate of breathing had increased.

He did not betray either shock or any other response as she stood up from him, then turned and bent over him as she held his head, and put her head almost into his neck, breathing in, to find out more about him from his smell, and then moved to his hair and did the same there.

By then, his hand was touching her by her knee.

He hoped she would not feel his suddenly turbulent feelings, or his alarm, at what she was doing to him; not knowing how she could possibly *not* detect how he felt.

Finally, with a gentle exploratory touch to his relatively rough cheeks, unshaven for many hours now, and with a faint stubble easily detected on them, she thanked him, and then returned to her own seat, saying nothing.

He could read nothing from her expression, except that he had noted that her eyes had been closed while she had done all of that, and they were still closed. He began to feel alarmed at what he had felt within himself at her closeness and her familiarity.

He was unable to speak for some time after that. His mouth had gone dry.

He should not be here! But he could not go, either.

He waited expectantly for her to tell him what she was thinking and had learned. He found he was suddenly wide awake, curious and attentive to what she might think; what she had learned.

She said nothing for a few moments, seeming to digest what she had learned, then stood again, moved her chair back, then knelt in front of him, and up against the side of his legs with her hands up near his waist. He was not sure what to expect now.

She took first one of his hands, and then the other, and placed them on the sides of her own neck, inviting him to find out in the same way, about her.

He felt a moment of panic at the feelings that began to course through him. She must have felt the uncertainty, and trembling in his touch, and his reluctance to take such a large, personal and even intimate step.

He seemed loath to do anything, so she took his hand and moved it to her forehead and onto her eyebrows and nose, to encourage him, and to allow his hands to move across her face in the same way that she had explored his, as her hands fell to his legs.

His eyes followed his hands as he touched what he saw; beginning to realize that with his eyes open, he relied more upon them than upon what he was feeling.

He stopped, took a deep breath, closed his eyes, and went over her face again, much more slowly, realizing that with his eyes open, he had been unable to sense what he now could, about her.

He took much longer over it than she had, as he had to find out what his fingers and his palms could tell him, using his entire hand to sense her cheeks and the shape of her face; feeling its warmth, and then finding out the more important details, with a light touch of his fingers, as she had done with him. It took him much longer than it had taken her, and required several passes as she knelt there, feeling the changes in how he was approaching these things. He was just learning those skills that were familiar to her.

He knew what beauty was to look at, but now began to feel what beauty really was, and to confirm what his eyes had already told him about her, but without telling him everything.

It was not his eyes that told him what was important; it was his hands, his fingers, and his other senses. The eyes deceived!

Those who said that beauty was only skin deep... but that true beauty lay within, knew so much more than he would ever know about beauty. She, had both inner and outer beauty. He sensed that, rarely, no matter how unbearable the provocation, would an ungenerous word ever leave his lips to be directed at her.

It was almost as if he could read her very innermost thoughts from his touch, and that he gained as much from her through his fingers, as she had felt of him, through hers, as though both were laying their souls bare to discovery.

She was a contradiction in so many ways; weak in the body, relative to a man, as most women were, and yet strong, with an inner strength that all women had – stronger than he was, forward, yet vulnerable and shy, happy, yet unutterably sad.

He felt like crying.

He was startled to feel her warm breath on his hands now, just as she must have been able to feel his, on hers.

His hands moved to her neck again, and gently touched her exposed shoulders. He had already been able to see that she had on a gown that left her neck and shoulders largely uncovered, and revealed more of herself there, than her previous threadbare dress, which had a relatively high neck to it.

He moved his hands back to her jaw, feeling her flowing hair on the back of his hands, and then moved on to the soft skin of her face again, touching so gently between her nose and her lips as he explored there again for a brief moment, finishing off upon her lips, hovering there, going over and over them.

He had kissed her here not that long ago. He wanted to kiss her again, but it had to be at her invitation.

As his nervous hands left her face, she said nothing, but rose higher on to her knees as she reached out and gently pulled his head into hers, just beneath her ear, so that he might smell her, as intimately and as revealingly, as she had earlier smelled him.

Now, he began to feel nervous.

With that encouragement, he moved, as she had done, to smell her hair, and then went on, to her exposed shoulder and the join of her shoulder with her neck, which she had not done with him, and back to her neck again. He began to feel alarmed at what he began to feel for this young woman.

She felt his nervousness, and smiled in understanding, as she returned to her seat. Neither said anything for a while. The air between them was too charged for speech.

She had probably felt the same way he'd felt.

There was so much that needed to be said, but so much that could not be said, just yet.

He was the first to move. He reached out and took her hand in both of his; feeling her sob, almost undetected, perhaps in relief over something as she placed her other hand on his. It was not so very dark where they sat, that he did not see a tear, and then another, start from her eyes. He did not understand what had happened, and yet, he did. They had just formed another bond, holding them together. He touched them away, smoothing his fingers over her cheek.

She sensed that she had shocked him in a strange way by what she had dared; no, had needed to do, just as he had shocked her in turn.

She had been concerned that he might not be able to forgive her for being so bold on such short acquaintance or being so firmly demanding – she had given him little choice – the same from him. But she had never been close to any man before except her father and brother, and this new feeling that she was encountering for the first time with this man, was very different. He was not like them at all, and this moment must not be wasted or let go.

His gentle touch let her know that he had forgiven her.

After that, it began to seem so easy that they would be able to speak in a more relaxed way, having discovered an understanding, however fragile or uncertain between them.

He found that he was anxious to relate his own history to her, wanting her to know everything about him, and he was interested to learn of her in the same way too, though that might be moving too quickly.

They sat forward in their respective chairs, close to each other, pulling them closer together again as before, to touch and to hold hands.

He spoke about himself at first.

She listened to him trying to explain to her about the sea-shore, and walking through the softly yielding sand without shoes on, feeling the sand between one's toes, not at all comfortable, and how, if you looked straight out to sea, there was nothing to see to the horizon except endless water.

She could not readily understand what she had not seen, as her first memories did not extend that far.

She had never been to a play, or heard an organ play in church.

The thought of what an orchestra might sound like, bewildered her. The thought of so many combined instruments would be so loud as to drown out the music. But then she recalled that she had fleetingly heard a small string ensemble when she had returned home with her father one evening and had driven by the assembly hall, and had heard one, amidst all of the revelry, and the raised happy voices from the people there.

Various plans formed in Robert's mind, and were thrown aside as too ambitious, too soon, too dangerous for her, or just plain, impractical daydreaming on his part.

But they did not totally disappear.

She laughed easily when he related some of the more humorous aspects of his childhood. She was not sure that she could believe that he could put chickens to sleep, or could call a rabbit from its burrow. She had never climbed a tree, nor understood why anyone might choose to do so. She had never caught a fish, or collected tadpoles, and was not sure that she knew what they were. She wondered what it might feel like to lie out in the pasture as he had done, and listen to the skylarks chirping high in the sky overhead, and then watch as they dropped like a stone down toward their nest.

She fell more serious when he related other incidents in his life that were perhaps more memorable because of the pain involved, when he had fallen out of a tree and broken his collar bone.

He was careful to avoid speaking of the recent, mind-filling, and unpleasantly disturbing memories of the last few years that still filled his waking and sleeping hours; the noise; the cold; the stink of death; the rats; the fleas; the disease. The death of friends! Many, many friends! But those other memories faded a little further into the background as the much more pleasant and immediate memories that began to be built up brick by brick, stone by stone, began to nudge those others aside.

The hours flew by. Neither of them noticed that James had entered the room on several occasions and had seen them sitting there, both, with their eyes closed as they spoke and laughed together, as they touched hands, or their foreheads had come together, so engrossed were they with each other.

He had never seen Miss Rebecca so happy, contented, or so relaxed.

Where am I?

Some time later, Robert awoke to hear others speaking above him. He lay still and listened. They were speaking of him, but he did not know why.

"Is he ill, James? I cannot tell. His brow is not heated, and he seems to be very relaxed and is breathing easily."

He felt a woman's soft touch on his forehead, but neither the touch nor the voice was Rebecca's.

"There is a small stain of blood here, on his shirt, high up, just under the edge of his coat! Can you be sure the wine was not drugged, James?"

"It was not drugged, Miss. I am aware of what your mother does behind our back, and it was a fresh bottle, unopened. If I suspect any of the wine being tampered with, then I make sure your mother gets that one, and a taste of her own medicine. Then we can be sure that she will not wander after that to torment any of us. No, he was very tired, and has been pulled around too much by those damned sawbones. Exhausted in fact. It showed on his face, along with the pain, so a little opiate would not come amiss, I think.

"He's just back from abroad miss, and also just out of Greenwich military hospital."

Robert recognized James's voice.

"I checked a moment or two ago, and it is an old wound that is proving difficult to heal fully. He must have opened it up a little last night. Nothing too serious. There is probably something still left in there that the surgeon could not find, and that is still working its way out. I put a little brandy on a cloth while he slept and kept it clean. He never stirred when I did that, and had he been awake I doubt he would have had anything kind to say to me over that. It's stopped bleeding now."

Robert struggled to sit up, and opened his eyes. A heavy cushion had been placed behind him, with another to rest his head upon. As he moved his legs, he noticed that his boots had fallen over as he had kicked them. He had not taken them off. Someone else had, but he had known nothing of it, and had not woken up. His coat had also been undone and his collar unbuttoned. He noticed a slight smell of brandy about himself, in keeping with what James had said.

Obviously, he had not left the house the previous night, as he should have done, but had fallen asleep in the chair, exhausted both physically and emotionally. What would they think of him? Rebecca was nowhere to be seen. He missed her presence. He had not intended to stay, or to fall asleep as he must have done, but he had been so overcome by tiredness.

He may have been sitting in a chair, sleeping, but he could not remember spending such a pleasantly restful night, though he cannot have slept long. What must Rebecca have thought of him, falling asleep in her presence like that?

He could see that it was not Rebecca that stood above him, but another young woman. Indeed there were two of them and he was seeing double. He closed his eyes. He must be in a worse state than he realized. It was also daylight, with the sun rising higher in the sky, and he could feel the warmth beating down from the roof above them The brighter image of the sun outside of the curtains showed that the day was advancing into late morning. He was still in the wingback chair he had been sitting in the previous evening.

He heard another voice slightly behind him, and recognized George's voice.

"You shouldn't have drunk any of that wine, Robert. It sneaks up on you and has a kick like a mule."

"He had but the one glass, Sir! Miss Rebecca drank more than that. She alerted me to him still being here, and fast asleep. She was worried for him. I had not the heart to waken him. She must have seen to him getting more comfortable and taking his boots off even, and would have stayed with him, but I persuaded her against that, and told her to get herself to bed."

He addressed Robert. "How are you feeling sir?"

Robert found his tongue. "I think I slept longer, and more restfully than I have slept for the last four months, but I do not remember falling asleep."

James noticed that his eyes seemed much brighter than they had been, and he was more alert, but then he had rested.

"We thought that it was time to get you awake. Besides, the girls were getting worried that you were sleeping too long. Fortunately, Mrs. Deming is gone for a few hours on some last-minute impulse, so we can go into the main part of the house without fear of encountering her. The servants know all about you being here.

"When she returns in a few hours, I shall get a full report from her coachman as to where she went and what she did. She does nothing that we do not know of. We bypass all of her efforts when we can, if we are careful."

George spoke "Can I take it that you are you well enough to leave, Robert, or that you will be, after a late breakfast? A very late breakfast."

His friend nodded as he rose to his feet and cautiously stretched the stiffness from his joints. The pain was less now than it had been when he had dared do that before.

"We can leave out of the front door this time. Mother is out! I shall escort you home. You should take this. "He passed him one of his gloves. "You must have dropped it last night. Mama discovered it in the corridor. That, is why I could not join you and we could not leave as we had planned. She was ready to tear the house apart from top to bottom to uncover some plot that she thinks my father and I have hatched between us, or to find the floozy she thinks I may have hidden away somewhere. To her, all soldiers are dissolute, and shambling liars, who left their morals entirely on the battlefield.

"We have time to relax for a while. She had some distance to go I think, and we will have enough warning when she returns. She did not take her maid with her, so she is up to something."

He watched his friend pull on his boots and straighten his clothing.

"Afterward, I will walk to your house with you and we shall talk in peace without fear of being overheard, or being forestalled, but I am told by my sisters and James, that I must leave this house, and preferably today, for my own safety, and theirs. I have had enough of her moods and hysteria anyway. I think Mama is a little more mad than usual."

He chuckled. "She feels she is being blocked at every turn in some subtle way by us, and by the servants too, but now she is beginning to see it, so she is becoming more crafty and even more dangerous, if that were possible. She is about to become desperate and possibly dangerous for us all, as well as herself. I shall go to my Grandmother's I think. She always welcomes me."

As they were getting ready to leave the house, and while George was getting the last of his few belongings packed away to send to his grandmother's house, James put a small slip of paper into Robert's hand.

"Miss Rebecca wrote you a message, sir." He saw the questioning look on Robert's face.

"She can write, Sir. Her father made a little wooden contraption for her that she can follow easily enough. She can do more, I think, than so many people who have their sight, but is denied the means to do so for the moment. That, will soon change I think."

It would, if Robert had his way, but then, none of what he would like to see happen might be possible. His mind was running off far beyond where it should be.

Robert put his hand on James arm and spoke quietly so that they could not be overheard. He had a concerned look in his eyes.

"You asked me last night what my intentions are toward Miss Deming, Rebecca." His eyes burned into the old man's and showed sudden anguish.

"I can answer you more honestly now, where I could not earlier, as I did not know, myself. I do now!"

He swallowed. "I am afraid! I am not safe for her! I had no feelings left in me when I first came here last night. Now, everything is turned about. Suddenly, I have too many feelings." He was pale.

"I am probably the biggest threat she might ever face, and I do not know what I am to do about it. If I were to hurt her, I would kill myself, and save you the trouble. It were better for her, and myself, if I do not come here again I think!"

He was surprised to find that James was smiling upon him. "There, there, sir! That is the best, and most honest answer of all. It was direct from the heart. The one I would not have tolerated was one in which you protested that you would be immune to her gentle ways, and that she would be entirely safe in your company. I would have known that to be an outright lie, and that you were hiding your real purpose, and denying your own feelings. From what I saw and heard last night as you both sat together as you did, and knew nothing of my comings and goings, it has gone beyond that. However, I fear that this is not about you, any more. But about her. I doubt you will be so easily able to stay away."

Robert knew that to be true! Everything that he did from this moment forward, and for the rest of his life, would be for her, yet he did not know how he would accomplish any of what he would like to do.

James continued. "I should not tell you this but I will. You had as devastating an effect on her last night too as she did on you, perhaps more so. I could see, that, as the evening unfolded, and then as it began to get light. She laughed more than I have heard her laugh before."

He smiled. "You, Robert, may not be safe in her company now, and not the other way around. You are afraid of hurting her, and that is a good sign. You will know how to behave."

Robert could scarce believe what he was hearing.

"Once Miss Rebecca knows what she wants, nothing will stop her easily. She and I had a long talk while you slept. She has some unusual views on many things, and is not afraid to be outspoken, though I tried to caution her. I sent her off to bed some hours ago, and Miss Helen came up and kept an eye on you, and then Miss Margaret came too; the twins. Aye, the girls are back.

"They began to suspect what their mother might be up to, and their father saw them return late last night. Their mother does not know yet. I kept them away from you both, as long as I could, but it was difficult until after Miss Rebecca retired, and they had spoken with her.

"Read that note, Sir. We shall see you again before long – even tonight - and then we shall talk again about something much more important, and I will require some other answers from you too. Answers to some very personal questions. We must decide how to go forward, and soon, but now I think we can." He sighed.

"It is going to be a very busy day!"

A Visit after dark.

Just after dusk of that same evening, Robert returned to the Deming Mansion. Ensuring that no-one would see him, he easily clambered into the tree outside of the garden wall, even in the dark. The branches had been carefully shaped for climbing. He maneuvered onto the wall, and then lowered himself to stand on the seat back, beneath him in the dark garden.

He heard a laugh next to him as he clambered down, recognizing that Rebecca was waiting for him on the lawn, even guiding his feet down, as he found the seat to stand on, before stepping to the ground.

"As you can see, James was right! I did return!"

"I knew you would, that you could not resist my written plea. Did your servants not miss you, with you being out all night?"

"No! They do not know my habits yet. I have been in the city for only two days. I told them never to worry about me. That I could look after myself, and I have my stick with me to defend myself from footpads.

"They are, however, striving to see that I put on weight again. They have been feeding me well, once I awoke from my afternoon nap. I think I am strengthening and putting on flesh again already. They were relieved to see me return from abroad. They had worried about me for the last few years.

"I told them not to wait up for me tonight, but that I would try to be home before first light this time, so you must make sure that if I am so ill-mannered as to fall asleep again while you are speaking, that you wake me up and send me packing."

"I hoped you would come. I was waiting for you."

He needed to hear that.

He felt her next to him, and then felt her take his hand as they sat down together, leaning his stick up against the seat. He had not brought either gloves or his hat with him, for fear of losing them, and alerting her mother to his presence.

"How could you be sure it was me, that was clambering over there, and not some other nefarious character with sinister purpose?"

He felt her take his arm into hers. "Some other, nefarious character indeed!" She found that funny.

"I knew it was you, approaching! Many small things that all added together. I heard you walking along the street some moments ago and recognized your footsteps. Then I heard your cane rattle against the tree as you climbed. I also heard a slightly indrawn breath as you suffered a moment of pain as you pulled yourself onto a higher branch." She laid each clue out in turn. "I knew it was you.

"Then, I recognized the smell of liniment on your hands, as well as a more masculine smell; unique, I think, to you. They all added up to you! I do not think you have any sinister purpose in being here, but I don't care anyway. James did not think so either, or he would not have given you my note, or the ribbon."

He felt her lean closer into him as she brought her feet up to the bench in front of her. He could vaguely see her bare feet again, as she wiped some grass off them. She was in the same dress she had first been in; the one she wore when she was out in the garden.

"Were you able to read my note? Was it clearly enough written?"

"It was very well written, and clear. As you can see, I accepted your invitation."

"I am glad! I ate well, earlier, but James has promised us some tea and cakes while we talk, but he is not going to allow you to have any wine tonight. It had a strange effect on you last night. You deserted me for the arms of Lethe, and quite forgot about your earthly cares. You abandoned me for her, but I do not resent that. I see that you did not forget me after all, as those who drank of her waters were destined to do. I was talking at great length as I am prone to do, and I realized that you had fallen asleep. You also snore, but so very gently. I found it all so charming, though I do not think you intended to fall asleep."

"Sleep, was the furthest thing from my thoughts, but it still caught up to me. Were you the one who took off my boots?"

"Yes, I did. I also unbuttoned your coat, and the button on your collar. Everything seemed so tight about you, and then I realized that you were still bandaged, and that I must trespass no further."

What else would she have done?

"I also put cushions behind you, or you would have awoken with a very stiff neck. I would have stayed with you, but James told me that I must go to my bed. My sisters had come back home, unexpectedly, and had gone straight off to their beds, but would be sure to pester me early, to ask about the gentleman that was with me."

She rested her head on his shoulder.

"Sure enough, they awoke very early and were clamoring to know where I was. They know how to get into my room when I am not there, which Mama does not - and they wished to speak with me. They knew where I had to be."

She readjusted her position, moving his arm around and behind her to give her more room.

"James said that he would see you got out of the house safely, and would try to keep my sisters from you for as long as he could, once they discovered my secret, which they soon did; that I had dined with a gentleman; a military friend of our brother, and that he was still here, and even sleeping. They couldn't stay away from you after that." She chuckled.

"They had to see you and meet you." She sighed ."They liked you, and even described you to me, and as each of them saw you.

"I slept well after that. Mama was out all day. She cannot get into my room to check whether or not I am there and I never answer to a knock. Those whom I do not mind, know how to get into my room without knocking. It makes her angry if she cannot get in, because then she does not know whether I am in a drugged sleep, as she intends, or am wandering about. I would rather she were angry outside of my door, than within it."

He listened, satisfied to hear her speaking, happy to listen to her, rather than have to speak, himself.

"I am glad you came back this evening, Robert. James was not sure that you would, thinking you would be too exhausted, though he contradicted himself almost immediately and admitted that he believed that it was quite certain that you would!"

"James is wise. I am not sure he approves of me. There are times I do not approve of myself."

She found that funny, along with so many other things he said. "What a strange thing to say."

"But, true. I fear I am not a good person. Society has a long memory, and is unforgiving."

He plucked up courage to ask a strange question.

"What do you, think of me, Rebecca?"

She hesitated, analysing it, debating whether or not she could answer.

"I know what I think, and what I feel, but I am not sure that I dare say, sir. Not at this moment. Not so soon."

He sensed that she might be blushing.

"No. I suppose not. I should not have asked." He would have had similar difficulty if she had asked him the same question about her.

She took his arm. "We should go inside, Robert. There are others wandering the street, and I would not like our conversation to be overheard. My sisters are very dear to me, but they are not above creeping close, to listen. Especially now that they know you are here with me, and would be coming tonight."

She drew him to his feet, leaving him hoping that she would move into his arms and request that he kiss her again, but she didn't. He may have rattled her with his question about what she thought about him.

She led him across to the house.

He tied the ribbon onto the branch that James had indicated, and then unlatched the entrance into the house.

The cloth she used, to wipe off the bottoms of her feet, had slipped off the projection that it had been put upon.

He retrieved if for her, telling her that he would do that simple thing for her. Before he closed the outer door, shutting off all light, little as there was, he suggested that she turn and sit upon a stair so that he could clean off her feet.

She sat as he requested, pulling her dress back onto her knees as he knelt in front of her, taking each foot in turn to clean it of any grass.

She rested her hand on his shoulder as he held her ankle. She may have felt him tremble as he touched her so familiarly, and with him seeing far too much of her for his comfort in the dim light, even indistinctly glimpsed under the edge of her dress, pulled out of the way just as on the first time, but not in a reflection this time, and much closer.

She may have heard him groan.

She was trembling herself because of his touch.

He wanted to reach out and find out more about her there in those fine hairs, but must not.

She left her hand on his shoulder after he had finished, not letting him rise, then took pity on him bringing him to her. She kissed *him*, this time. He responded, moving even closer, becoming trapped between her legs, his body, moving her dress far up along her upper legs to her body as they kissed again. She stroked his hair and tried to pull him closer, encouraging him. But to do what? He could feel her body, just as she could feel his.

He was a lost man.

She did not pull back from him. She couldn't, but she didn't complain either about what she could feel of his body, telling her how excited he was for her, if she knew what that meant, and she must know.

He let out a long breath and slowly pulled back from her, but not wanting to.

"That, is why you must not trust me, my… my, Rebecca."

She said nothing.

He hung that cloth where it should be, and they climbed to the upper level, with him holding on to the bottom of her dress as she carried his stick for him.

Steady progress.

If he lost touch of her, she paused to let him find her leg, and to learn again where she was, and then proceeded even more slowly.

On the upper platform, they exchanged places, coming too close to each other again as they did so. He was still a disgrace to his sex, and she must know it, could feel it against her.

He pulled the section of wall inward as they carefully maneuvered to avoid it, her arms around him, pulling him into her, not caring about anything, to make as small an obstacle as possible, then turned with him again.

He pushed his stick out onto the attic floor, then strove to give her enough room to get out ahead of him, his head, swimming with what he was learning about her.

When she was alone, she could easily do it for herself, but with him so close behind her, it was not easily done. She was too close to the wall and her dress snagged on projections, stopping her climbing.

She hesitated. "When I am alone, I have no difficulty with this, I can bunch…" She left him with the thought that she could 'bunch' her dress up, and climb, unhindered. It was a thought that tormented him. She had been tormenting him a lot, recently.

"I will lift you." He stooped and lifted her, helping her by wrapping his arm around her legs below her knees, yet under her dress, so that his arm would not slip on the material, and to save her from climbing, too close to the wall, and possibly bruising her knees. His face was pushed into her, behind her.

He lifted her to lie out on the floor on her front, ahead of him, in a reversal of how they had come into this space that time before, then she turned to sit in front of him; her dress, askew and above her knees again her legs far apart for balance, revealing even more, even in that less-dim light, than he had first seen of her reflected in that glass, or downstairs, just moments earlier.

The 'hits' were coming at him too frequently. His mouth was dry.

She straightened her dress, saying nothing of that revealing moment, though she must know of it, and moved herself back from the opening, creating just as much of a problem for him with what he could still see as she inched back ahead of him.

He might not survive any more of this.

He followed her; pulled the section of wainscoting back to latch behind them, and then clambered to his feet with her help.

He noticed that there was a candle burning on the table, and that the curtains were already closed. He saw then, that she had on an older dress very similar to the one she had first worn the previous night, but this one did not have an ink stain upon it. It was shorter than the other one, and he could see her bare feet clearly beneath it.

They sat, as before, facing each other, recovering their senses over what had happened; both, still flustered with those kisses, and everything else that had happened between them.

"James is here." She'd heard him approaching.

At that moment, James entered the room, bearing a tray. He had heard them enter that door downstairs. Robert had not been aware of his approach, but Rebecca had.

"Good evening, Robert. I take it you are not as ill as we feared this morning?"

"Much recovered, thank you."

"I knew you had arrived when I heard your voices in the garden when I put my head out of the door, and then I saw that ribbon as you came upstairs."

He had wasted no time following them into the house.

"You need not worry about your mother tonight, Miss. I saw that her glass of wine was from the same bottle she had intended to leave for you with your dinner, but I took it away, and gave it to her with her own dinner. You may have a peaceful few days, until she suspects what we are doing, though I constantly stay a few steps ahead of her."

He set a teapot and cups beside them, in a carefully arranged manner, and a plate of cakes.

"Is Papa home, James?"

"No miss. He is still out."

James poured the tea for them both, and put the teapot back, exactly where it had been, with the handle in the same position.

"I think he was relieved that George is over at his grandmother's house now. That is one worry, less for him to deal with.

"He said he would not be home too late. He still has to read the gazette to you, and will continue that book of poems, and those others too, if he has time, though now that Robert is here…." He left that thought unfinished.

"He gave me this one to bring up when I came up here again. It is one he picked up yesterday. The poems of Robert Burns! He warned me to let you know that some of them are a little 'daring', if you know what I mean?"

She laughed gently.

"Your name-sake, Robert! A good omen! Yes. I know what you mean by 'daring', James. I am familiar with Mr. Burns.

"After we have had some tea and this cake, I will ask Robert, if he would not mind reading some of them to me." She paused. "That is, if you will not be embarrassed by some daring poetry. Mr. Burns had quite a reputation with the ladies, but it was all honest emotion, I think. They knew better than to expect constancy, or any attachment from him.

"I can understand his emotional feelings, better than I can deal with Byron's shameless, unfeeling, morals, which were far from being honest, or even forgivable! But I think I would like first to hear his 'ode'—I think it was an 'ode'—upon a mouse: that one with:

'Wee timorous, cowering, beastie!'

"Or perhaps the one on seeing a louse on a lady's bonnet in church. A religious louse, no doubt! I love the last few lines of that poem:

'Oh would some power, the giftie, gie us…'

"Oh dear. I hope I do not seem too bookish for your liking, Robert? Perhaps you do not like poetry, or reading aloud to anyone, or, an over- educated woman?"

He quickly re-assured her.

"Far from it! You are charming, and unexpectedly entrancing, my dear."

It slipped out before he could stop himself, hearing her chuckle at his daring to address her that way. However, he did not break his stride.

"My mother was far better-educated than my father, and he was proud of her for it. She saw that I was not neglected for poetry, or good writing of any kind. If I recall, Burns then continued:

'Oh would some power, the giftie, gie us…

to see ourselves as others see us.'

"They are sobering considerations, those lines."

She had been speechless for a few seconds and then laughed gently.

"Did you hear that, James? He can not only recite, Burns, but he called me, My Dear? There is hope for me yet!"

She could not see his blushes, but realized that he must be blushing.

"I am sorry!" He stammered in response. "I forgot myself, and where I am. That slipped out!"

She would not accept that.

"Do not apologize, Robert, or I will think that you are the *timorous beastie*. You were not timorous at all when you helped me earlier on the stairs, but were very forthright with what needed to be done. You even know, Burns!"

She clapped her hands like an excited little girl.

"Oh, I think we shall get on famously now! But I already knew that. Now, have some cake, Robert, and the tea, and then we can begin.

"If you find my name... Rebecca, a mouthful, you can keep calling me, 'my dear'. I do like that! No one could possibly object to that, I hope."

James retreated with a smile on his face. He would check on them in an hour or two and see if they needed anything else. He had no fear about leaving Miss Rebecca alone with him now, even though the situation had become more precarious for Robert with the way she would be likely to torment him in her innocence.

All James had to focus upon, was keeping her sisters from pestering them unmercifully if they knew he'd arrived and was with their sister.

Visitors were never welcome in this house, unless they were special friends of their mother, and they, were few and far between. Men, young men especially, were never welcomed.

"Now, Robert, you shall move over and allow me to share that chair with you if you do not object. No-one needs chairs so big and that put us so far apart, after what we learned of each other yesterday."

He moved over, as she suggested, and felt her squeeze in beside him without any concern about anything.

"I am not crushing you am I, or hurting your shoulder?"

"I am comfortable."

"Good!"

She brought her feet up onto the chair and leaned into him as she re-arranged her dress, pulling at it and adjusting it for greater comfort for her as she moved her legs around, without nearly as much concern as she did that, as there should have been.

He began to read to her, with her legs leaning over, onto his own.

She reached down and took his arm from under her and moved it behind her back so that they had a little more room for her to snuggle closer to him, and so that he would have his arm about her as he read to her.

She brought her feet even more under her, moving her skirt back from her knees to stop it tearing.

"You may rest the book against my legs, Robert, and you will need only one arm. I will turn whatever pages that need to be turned, when you tell me. You can begin with, 'the mouse', which he turned up in the field he was plowing. I hope you can sound like Burns with his broad accent."

"I should be able to. My mother was also from Ayrshire."

"How famous!"

He began.

'Wee, sleekit, cow'rin', tim'rous beastie....'

She listened for a while after he'd finished, as they both thought about what he'd read to her. She repeated some of the lines.

"'*The best laid schemes of mice and men, gang aft agley*.' How true that is! For both the good schemes, and the ill ones, I think.

"'*The present only, toucheth thee*'. True again. It is the past which most haunts us."

He knew that to be true!

She seemed suddenly to be quite sad. He tightened his arm about her to provide some comfort, placing his free hand over her legs, and turning his face into her hair, feeling her snuggle even closer into him.

Her arm moved across his body, and held him, even as his lips brushed her forehead.

"I think, if you do not mind Robert, that we can leave the louse poem for later, and just sit like this for a while."

"We can do that, my dear."

He felt her hand touch his own, and then explore his fingers. He smiled, recognizing what she needed to learn.

"No, my dear Rebecca. I have no wedding ring. I am not married. Neither am I engaged, nor am I promised or even sought after." He chuckled.

"James would never have allowed me near you if I was any of those."

"How did you know what….?" She was startled to recognize that he knew what she had been finding out.

He continued. "Nor do I have any women of consequence in my life except for one very special young woman whom I just met, and possibly her two sisters who seemed concerned for my health this morning, but there is only one of them that interests me, and that I would always like to kiss, and she is sitting by me now... and I am moving forward far too quickly!"

He said it all in one breath, recognizing how he had let his thoughts run away with him.

"You are not moving too quickly for me, Robert. Look how we are sitting; as though we were lovers, and had been lovers for ever."

She did not seem to mind making that suggestive comment.

"Thank you for not being too shy with me. Now I am sure I am blushing at having been found out. You seem able to read my mind." She kissed him on his cheek.

"I do not need to read your mind, my dear, I just need read my own."

He kissed her on the forehead in return, and felt her snuggle even closer to him, deeper in the chair and in his arm, and turn her face up to him to invite, and then to receive their next kiss.

He did not deny her, or himself, but was gentle about it, as she deserved. He saw a slight wetness on her cheeks. Her arm rose around his neck, holding him close to her.

"What I feel here, inside, of my own feelings, Rebecca, seems to be exactly what I believe you must feel too. I hope so. It is intoxicating, as well as strengthening, and maybe even alarming!" He took several breaths.

"I cannot remember ever having such feelings before for anyone, as I have now for you. I feel as though I would never like to leave this place, and every time I do go – all of one time now; except that I left you when I fell asleep in the early hours of just this morning – it is as though I should never have left."

"You felt it too." She had known the same feeling.

"I do not want you to leave either, Robert, ever, and yet you will, because you must." She was breathing heavily for someone who should be calm and in control.

"Can this be happening so quickly to two people, Robert? To us?"

"I believe it did, my dear."

"Yet…" she seemed unable to say something that needed saying.

"Yes, my love?" He tried to encourage her.

She detected that change in expression, but did not object to his boldness.

"No; it is too soon to say anything of that. Love, is perhaps a step too far at this moment. I must just be satisfied with what is in the 'now', and learn to be happy with whatever I can grasp at any one moment in time.

"Like that little mouse, I must learn to live only in the present. There might not be a future for me in that way. I cannot have a normal future like that enjoyed by other people. I must take happiness as I can find it, wherever that is, and however fleeting it may be."

Uncertainty?

He was not sure about this uncertainty she was expressing, but thought he knew where it came from; her own fears. He could help her with those.

"I think I can dare to promise you, that there will be a future for you, my Rebecca, if I have my way. Your happiness will not be fleeting, or just... of-the-moment. You are more normal, and more deserving, than anyone I have ever met."

She cautioned him. "You do not know me that well, Robert."

He tried to re-assure her, disturbed by her fear of what lay ahead of her.

"I know what I know. We will gradually find out the rest about each other. You do not know me, either."

"But you know nothing of us, Robert. You know nothing of this dysfunctional family, of the difficulties with Mama, or how she rules everything with an iron hand or makes everyone's life a total misery, in proportion to the resistance she encounters.

"It was bad enough before George returned, but then it grew worse. He was unwise enough to criticize and resist her and argued at first, over what he saw and believed. I think he had forgotten, or did not know, what she might be capable of."

Robert pushed into her neck and stroked her face, touching her lips with his fingers as he leaned in to kiss her upon them once more.

"I know much more than you think, Rebecca. Your brother and I spoke for an hour or more as he walked with me, to be sure I got home safely this morning."

He sighed heavily. "But let us not dwell on unpleasantness, but on something else that I have been thinking about."

She waited for him to continue.

"There is a church, not so far distant from here." He felt her glance up at him, suddenly holding her breath, concerned at what he might suggest, but also, excited.

"Tomorrow evening, there is an organ recital there, by a very accomplished and well-known organist. He is to play some of the compositions of J. S. Bach, and George Friderick Handel. If I could smuggle you out of the house, and get you back safely again, would you go with me?"

"How could I do that, Robert?"

"If you but say, yes, and James is agreeable—though God knows why he would be—I would see to everything and see you safe. You would not be recognized!"

She thought for a few moments.

"If James agrees, then I would be pleased to go with you, though how you would get him to agree so easily, or so soon; or how you will manage it, I am at a loss to understand."

"That, is all I ask of you, my love. Just leave it to me, and, hopefully we shall go, and not encounter a louse upon a lady's bonnet there."

"Thank you, Robert."

She kissed him under his ear and hugged him even more tightly than before, as he continued with the second of the Burn's verses she had been interested in; putting his arm back over her legs to pull her closer to him as she settled even lower into the seat, though that soon changed with her moving her legs over his arm, which then was touching the back of her legs, but changing all of the time as she continued to move to get herself more comfortable.

As he read, he became more and more conscious of a tickling sensation on the back of his fingers, as well as warmth as she moved closer to him, relaxing even more.

His hand was where it should not have been.

He knew exactly where he was, and what he was touching, with her lower body under her dress, pushing into his hand, yet she was saying nothing, still snuggling into him and moving her legs around to get herself ever more comfortable.

There was no complaint from her that he was touching her so intimately, and he did not want to change anything, though touching her like that affected him strongly.

He did not remove his hand from under her dress, as he knew he should do, nor did he try to discover any more about her, as he ached to do, but continued reading to her as she relaxed upon his hand; always pushing closer into him, always bringing him closer to her has she took his arm by his elbow and pulled at it to touch her where, and as she wanted him to touch her.

He wouldn't have to move at all. She was presenting herself openly to him, even in semi-consciousness (if she was semi-conscious), moving her legs, and moving them farther apart to provide more space for him to touch her ever more intimately, and to discover more... or even to...!

Then, she reached over even farther, between her legs, moving her dress higher upon her legs, and rested her hand upon him; that aroused part of his, standing up within his clothing. She did not go any further than that, just resting her hand there, sensing his feelings and his mood for her, bringing him even more to life. They had moved lifetimes, in as many days. He was breathless, but somehow, maintained control as he read.

His mind, and hers too-- if the truth were known-- were everywhere else than upon Robert Burns' poetry at that moment, or dwelling upon *'a louse on a lady's bonnet in church'*.

At the end of reading it, he paused, waiting for her to say something, perhaps even to object to what he was touching and sensing of her body, and what it was doing to him. He was too excited, and not far from losing himself, and that must not happen where he was.

She closed herself upon his hand, bringing her legs tightly together, trapping him, and at the same time she groaned as she sighed heavily, becoming even warmer and moister, even wet, upon his hand.

If he turned just a little into her.... If he were free... he could just... push, as she seemed to be encouraging him to do.

The thought overwhelmed him.

She must know what was happening to him. To them.

Neither of them said a word, with those verses filling their thoughts and other feelings beginning to flood over them both, about what they could feel and sense of each other as he touched and caressed her. At least he knew exactly what his own feelings were, and they were rapidly moving beyond his control.

A proposition.

"That, was entertaining and charming."

The voice came out of the dark behind them, from the doorway. It was James.

Robert's feelings had very nearly got away with him. He fought to bring them back under control, removing his hand slowly from beneath Rebecca's dress, tangled up in his emotions as he had been touching and caressing her there. He pulled at her dress to bring it to cover her as he slowly recovered his wits and changed his position with her, sitting up.

Thank god the room was dim.

Fortunately, James had not just entered the room and walked straight over to them before he'd spoken.

"If I mistake not, young mistress is asleep there with *you* now, instead of the other way about. She never was able to settle at this time of night in any comfort, so she must feel secure with you, and in this room too."

He also took in the relaxed manner of her sitting there with her legs up beside, and even over him, and her arm across him, while one of his was around her, and the other across her legs too, just under the edge of her dress, pulling at it to cover her.

He said nothing. He was pleased to see that she trusted him enough to go to sleep in his arms, as she had, but it was getting late, and he should be going home.

She needed someone other than her own sisters and father to lean on, and to depend upon. He began to feel hope for her where he had previously felt only hopelessness and despair, wondering how he might help and protect her, and how things might move forward without destroying the one part of this family that would need protecting the most, though it was all, dear to him.

This young man coming into her life, had now presented them with that possibility.

Robert turned his head to look at Rebecca, and saw that she was indeed asleep. She had not be totally conscious of what had been happening between them. He was sorry for that. It would have propelled their relationship along much more quickly and with a deeper understanding of their emotions for each other.

As his warm breath passed down across her face, she sighed and pushed her head deeper into his shoulder, reaching out to take his hand and began to move it under her dress once more to where it had been, and where she wanted it to be again.

It was reassuring, but Robert had to resist that, with James coming closer to them. He may already have seen too much.

He dragged his mind onto something else that was almost as important.

"James…?"

He faltered wondering how he might go about asking something that would seem entirely outrageous to anyone, especially as Rebecca and he, had known each other for such a brief span in time.

James patiently waited for him to continue.

"…Miss Rebecca said that if I could gain your approval for something I suggested to her, that she would be happy to accept my suggestion! Presumably, otherwise, not!"

"What suggestion was that, Robert?"

At least he'd dropped this formality of calling him, 'Sir', all of the time.

Robert was pleased to see that James had never regarded him as anything but an equal, and had been outspoken in everything he had said in protection of Rebecca.

Robert would be the same now, just as outspoken. Life was too brief to lose any part of it in equivocating.

"I told her of an organ recital at the Cathedral, not so very far from here tomorrow evening, and I offered her my escort and protection if she would like to go."

He added a little more of a description. "For Rebecca, an organ recital would be an experience of the hearing, and of the mind. She has hearing sensitivity and feeling far beyond that of anyone I have ever met."

"I heard of that recital too, Robert, but had not thought of it in quite that way, or with any particular reference to Rebecca. But yes. I know she would enjoy that, difficult as it is for any of those in this house to get her there."

"It is for tomorrow evening. A program of Bach and Handel."

Robert hesitated. "Perhaps it is too early to make such a suggestion, and I must seem far too ambitious, encroaching, even dangerous. I am also not sure that I should be trusted by anyone (especially after what had just been happening). I am a complete unknown to all of you."

Miss Rebecca had become very attached to him in the last two days, and in a surprising way, showing not an ounce of shyness with him. Her excitement had been obvious to everyone around her.

"I offered to take her to it, but only with your approval. I would see to it that she came to no harm, and that she will be suitably dressed, with no chance of being recognized. I would bring her back, immediately after."

It seemed as though he were pleading on her behalf.

"I know it is very much to ask, but I would like to see that she might experience that, where she is denied so much in other freedoms."

His suggestion was not immediately blocked.

"How would she be dressed?"

All hope had not been dashed!

James continued. "I do not think that she has any suitable clothing for that kind of an adventure. How are you to get her there without a problem? What is more important is, how are we to avoid her mother, and keep her from suspecting her daughter is not in the house? Though she does not know from one minute to the next where Rebecca is anyway, so that is not a problem."

He was getting warmed up to the idea.

"I think we might also need her father's permission too. He has asked about you, and I know that he intends to meet you soon, considering what Miss Rebecca and the twins told him."

Another voice broke in.

"That meeting can be now, James!"

A tall man had entered the room, unheard and unseen in the relative darkness over by the door, until he spoke.

It was not clear how long he had been there, or what he might have overheard.

He took in the young couple sitting closely together in one chair; not sure that he entirely approved of their relaxed familiarity with each other on such short acquaintance, with his daughter's dress not fully covering her legs, though he said nothing about that, and in the relatively poor light, his face was not easily read.

He began to sense a revolution about to sweep through his household. If so, it was overdue, and none too early at that, but he would need to approve of it.

This was not the time to be difficult. This young man who had so captivated his daughter, may represent the opportunity he had long awaited, to deal with all that was ill in the household, and had been for several years, but which had been steadily getting worse by the week, and even by the day now, since his son had returned from the continent.

"No, do not disturb her! Let her rest."

He forestalled Robert moving from the chair to meet him properly and waking his daughter.

"She gets little enough rest in this house."

He realized that Robert had not been about to move, despite how the circumstance might look to another, but had been adjusting their positions to let his daughter rest more peacefully.

He smiled at the young man's protective attitude, matching what James had told him. It mirrored his own feelings.

The young man, Robert, seemed to know his own mind where Rebecca was concerned and was prepared to fight for her interests.

Mr. Deming did know something—perhaps too much—of this young man, and his history. Parts of it were worrisome, but he would find out more, before he judged.

"I am also interested in hearing an answer to those questions that James asked you, young man. How would you ensure her anonymity and safety?"

Robert spoke quietly, and as persuasively as he could. He had obviously given it a good deal of thought.

"She can be dressed, much as she is now, Sir, and with something on her feet. No one will see what she is wearing. I will bring a heavy cloak for her to wear. It used to be my mothers, and it will hide everything about her features and keep her warm.

"It has a large hood on it that will hide her features, and the light will be low where we will be.

"Leaving here, we will walk a little way from the house, and then my own coach will transport us, once we leave the house without being seen, and she will return the same way after the recital is finished. I shall be armed, and I well-know how to use my swordstick to good effect."

Mr. Deming had heard that, for himself, knowing it to be true. Mr. Hannan was not to be judged superficially, despite his war injuries.

Rebecca's father was silent as he digested what he had heard, weighing up the pros and the cons of the matter.

"You make it all sound so very easy, while we who are here find nothing easy. How long have you been planning this, I wonder? But you can undoubtedly succeed where none of us could."

He turned to James.

"If you can bring some cushions over James, we might be able to gently pry this young man away from my daughter's embrace and let her rest there in peace while we talk further about this."

He looked lovingly down at his daughter. He had a disturbing feeling, that if he were not careful, he would soon lose her, though not too easily, and not without a much better understanding of this man, but she needed to be got out of this house as soon as it could be arranged. She, or her mother would have to go.

It might happen anyway, and Rebecca would need to go, whether he was careful in his looking after her. or not. And with a better understanding of this young man, or not.

Some things had an existence of their own, as he had seen when he had first entered the room and listened. This had not been a stranger he had been listening to, but someone his daughter was already in love with. He began to hope for her, where he had not dared to hope before.

He had prayed this moment might come, but had feared both that it would, and that it might not. And here it was, and all because of an accident in her brother bringing this man to his home when he had. A relative stranger to them all, no less, but one that had upset everything in the merest blink of an eye!

Such a small event at the time, but already with almost unbelievable consequences, as he could see. His eyes did not deceive him as they usually did. It was an embrace of two young people who were at their ease with each other and were in love. He remembered that time well, himself.

He changed the subject before his feelings got out of control and he exercised the parental authority that demanded he say 'no', to this preposterous suggestion!

"I see she persuaded you to read some of that Burns to her. Unless she recited them to you. She knows most of them by heart, and that is how she entertains herself when she is alone if I or her sisters or brother are not with her and reading to her.

"She is also a great mimic. If you read any of them to her in Burns own brogue, then you might ask her to recite it back to you in the same way. I think her enunciation will surprise you."

He tapped his stick upon the floor in agitation and made up his mind.

"I think I am inclined to give you my permission young man, but you will need to persuade me further, and with more detail, for my better comfort with what you plan, and I need to know more of you, personally."

Robert explained to him as best he could, what he planned, to get Rebecca to that concert and back again, answering all of his questions.

They did not so much listen to him, as were weighing him up in the way he spoke, how he spoke, his body-language. His love for the girl, the young woman, in the chair beside him was clear for all to see. He was inclined to like him, and began to feel easier in his decision as time had slipped by.

"Both my wife and twin daughters have a social appointment in the city tomorrow evening. They, the twins, had initially decided not to go, which was quite putting their mother out, but now I think I shall persuade them otherwise, though I shall disclose as little of this as I can.

"Now, let us see if we can awaken my daughter with the least fuss, and persuade her that she should now retire. James and I will retreat and let you do that, sir, and then the twins can come in and see that she gets to bed.

"Tell her none of what we have decided. If she learns of that, tonight, she will never sleep.

"We shall see you, tomorrow evening, Robert."

"Good night, Sir."

Another daring and open conversation.

They'd dared to leave him alone again with her?

Robert could hardly believe it. They must know how he felt, and how he was affected by this wondrous young woman laid out along that chair, sleeping; helpless; still so openly vulnerable after what they had done.

They had said that the twins would soon join them, so he had better be on his best behavior and resist the temptations so easily within reach.

He should strive to be more worthy of their trust; of her trust.

He moved to sit by her again, replacing the cushions with his own body; turned into her, bringing her to lean against him, moving some hair back from her face, and kissed her full upon her lips. Her knees were drawn up to her, displacing her dress and opening her up to his discovery once more as he could see. Somehow, he resisted that overwhelming temptation.

She did not seem to want to be awoken, so he kept repeating those kisses, all over her face. If she did not wake up, then he might risk touching her again in that place he could see. That, would be sure to wake her up.

She complained in a low voice but did not push him away. Instead, she pulled him down to her again, mumbling, in her near-sleep, objecting to being disturbed, even while being disturbed so nicely by being kissed, but he was slowly getting through to her.

She reached up, more consciously awake now, and put her arms around his neck, pulling him down to her so that she knew where he was, relative to her, returning that kiss; those kisses, even eagerly, now that she was awake.

She was blushing, and even breathing in a strangely labored way, having been pulled from whatever dream had held her.

She turned onto her back beside him, still careless of where her dress was.

"Oh, Robert! It is, you. Thank goodness! I had the most interesting, shocking dream, and you were in it, speaking to me, reciting poetry. Burns, even as you were doing... other... strangely wonderful things, to me."

She broke off from that thought.

"You were reading poetry, just as you were when I went to sleep. At least, I think I was asleep; half, in, and half, out, of sleep anyway, but I am not sure I can, or should, describe what was happening between us." She was blushing.

Her agitation was obvious. Her hands drifted down on her body and she pushed her dress closer to her body between her legs as though to try and sense something about herself there, but without being too obvious about it, as she would be if she lifted her dress and put her hands under it to discover what she would like to know about herself, where she felt distinctly warm, and quite moist.

"It seemed so real, and it was all so very personal… and it was much more than kissing. Much more!" She seemed shocked.

She dared to continue.

"You were holding me, reading to me. We were very close, and… and… you were... touching me, in a special way."

"Yes, my love? Touching you in what, special way?"

"I was too warm, so I moved and… and…" She was avoiding telling him, in her embarrassment.

Robert took a deep breath and told her what had actually happened that she seemed so afraid to dwell upon, to save her from this agony of uncertainty that she was clearly beginning to recall, needing to know what had happened.

"Let me save you from saying any more, my love. You became conscious that I was touching you where I should not have been touching you, and in a very intimate and special place."

She buried his head into his shirt to hide her sudden look from him, and she nodded against him. He felt that.

"Yes, you were. You were touching me, between my...! But... and I should not admit this... but you were so gentle, and it was so very pleasant. I was not objecting as I should have been.

"I responded to your touch, Robert, and moved closer to you... down there... so that you could touch me even more, which I so wanted and needed you to do."

That admission alone was a shock for her to admit to, but he had helped.

"Robert. What have I become? What is happening to me? I fear I am not a nice person to admit to enjoying any of that, yet I did enjoy it. I liked being touched by you there."

He was encouraged enough to move his hand to touch her upon her knee, under her dress, startling her.

"It was not a dream you were having, my love. It was real. I was touching you under your dress. I touched, I caressed, and I wanted to do so much more to you. I would have done, was even ready to do so, but for James coming into the room."

She blushed, and chuckled nervously that he dared to admit to any of it. He was as bad as she was.

"You detected some of that about me, earlier, when I came closer to you on the stairs after I'd wiped off the bottoms of your feet, and our bodies came very close together.

"If you recall, I could not help myself, and I pushed closer into in my eagerness, moving your dress out of the way between us. I was aroused for you even then. I know you felt my excitement at that moment. I could not hide it. I will never be able to hide it from you. I am still that way, and probably always will be when I am close to you."

She'd noticed, but had resisted reaching out to discover that for herself.

He sighed. "Can you forgive me?"

She smiled; relieved that he was prepared to shoulder so much of the blame for what had happened. He could see that smile and was encouraged to continue speaking and to touch her a little farther up her leg, slowly encroaching upon where he wanted and needed to be.

She said nothing to stop him.

"So you see, Rebecca, we are equally to blame. We have that effect on each other."

She reached up and stroked his face.

"I think we shall have to forgive each other, Robert. I was not entirely innocent in any of that, as you know. I knew what I was doing, even if I didn't always understand why I did it, or what the consequences would be for me, or for you. I think I would like to know about those... consequences, provided I learn about them with you. I know you would be gentle with me."

She had to think about that; trying to understand herself, and the strange and wonderful changes that had happened in her life, and to her, since Robert had come into her life.

"I did feel you against me, Robert, though it is all very strange to me; things I never knew, and never experienced before. I did not know about such feelings until you caused them to grow within me.

"I think I know what you wanted to do to me, even then, though without understanding exactly what that was. I don't recall objecting to what you were doing, and I did not push you away as I think a moral young woman should have done."

"You didn't, my love. Though, as you say, you should have done."

"But why should I have pushed you away? I needed to know where that would lead, and I didn't want to object. I wanted to know more, and for you to teach me."

Her mind was busy, deciding how much to say, and how much not to say about how she felt.

"I think I would like to know more about these strange feelings I have. When I paused on the stairs in front of you after you'd lost your hold on the hem of my dress, I wondered if... if you would touch me more personally then; if you would put your hand up... under."

She sighed at that thought. She'd known even then that he wanted to.

"You did touch me, but only on the ankle and my leg, and not as I wanted. Then, when you helped me into this room, I had pulled my dress out of the way, intending that you would see what I wanted, and I was much more open for you then, to see, and even to touch, as I laid out in front of you with my dress above my knees, but you didn't. I decided then, that I would have to help you… get... over.... and even more... directly." Her words tailed off.

She admitted even more. "I was not totally asleep when you touched me as you did, but I gave you no choice about touching me like that. I also reached out like some bold harlot to touch you in turn?

"Where I found the courage...?"

He kissed her again.

"Yes, my love, you did, and that was very courageous. Thank you for startling me as you did. That, was very enervating for me."

"I felt how, enervating, Robert, when I noticed how you changed under my hand."

She reached up and kissed him.

"Oh, Robert. What does it mean? What does it say about me? About my dreadful character, that I placed all of that temptation before you so shamelessly, and encouraged you to touch me like that?"

He laughed.

"What does it say about me as a supposed gentleman, that I helped you and even responded to touch you? I didn't resist you. I didn't hold back. I would quite happily have undressed us both, there and then, and have had us coupling in this very chair where we are, except that I knew we would never be left alone together for long enough.

"James would have thrown me out into the garden from this very window; dragged out into the street and told never to come back again."

"I would have stopped him, Robert."

"Yes, I think you would.

"You and I, my love, are as alike as two peas in a pod. We each know what we want, and we are not afraid to go after it."

His words reassured her that any blame should be equally shared.

"But I instigated it, Robert, and I did it deliberately. I moved into you, I… lifted my dress out of the way… I encouraged you to touch me there."

He closed off those self-recriminations with a kiss.

"Thank you for having the courage to do that. You are amazing. I was a willing participant, don't forget. A more than willing participant. The same criticisms could be said of me. But what man could resist such beauty or such temptation to me, as you are. What it means, and says about us both, is that… and I will say it out loud and acknowledge it openly… is that we are in love, my dearest Rebecca, so do not feel guilty about anything. Everything we did, is what happens between two lovers. Though not usually so quickly as it did between us."

She fell silent. She liked that thought. Lovers! And that they would soon be actual lovers, the way things were going.

"Those openly-expressed feelings; wanting to be close to each other; wanting to kiss the other all of the time; wanting to touch everywhere one is allowed to touch of the other, and where one is usually not allowed to touch; to share everything; this chair, our thoughts and even, eventually, our bodies, are all signs of love, wanting to express itself."

"Our bodies." That thought intrigued her, wondering how that could be done. "Then we soon shall be lovers, Robert. Soon. I want to know what that really means, and how it can be achieved. But I hear the twins approaching, so you should not go under my dress and touch me so well again, as I ache for you to do, and as I know you want to do. You have been getting closer to doing that all of the time, you naughty boy, but I will not stop you."

His hand was even then beginning to touch upon her thigh, high under her dress, as her forgiving and encouraging words, and as her admissions seemed to encourage him to do.

"I may not survive these temptations, my love." He kissed her.

"You are not the only one, Robert. I know that I will not sleep tonight thinking about that, and about the organ recital tomorrow. I almost leapt out of the chair when I heard Papa say that he would give his permission for you to take me to that, but I knew that I should not wake up so suddenly, but must wait for them to leave so that you could wake me up, but, Robert, you did not wake me up in the way that I would have preferred, as in that dream that was not a dream."

He sighed heavily. "Now I definitely will not, survive. And now that I know what you want, my love, I shall be much more forward with you than I have been."

"Good." She snuggled closer to him, giving him permission, but aware of how little time they had.

At that moment, the twins, burst into the room, laughing excitedly, and ran over to them.

"Rebecca, what did you say to father?"

They paused, seeing the pair of them slowly moving apart in that chair, recognizing what they may have interrupted and seeing where Robert's hand had been under their sister's dress. They couldn't say anything about that in front of Robert, but would quiz Rebecca when they got her alone.

"We have never seen him so cheerful about anything. James too. We are here to escort you safely to your bed, and to let Robert know that he can leave through the house this time; Mama is in her bed, sleeping, after she drank that wine with her supper."

Robert leaned in to Rebecca, and whispered to her, not yet able to stand up without revealing too much of his condition to these far-too-observant sisters.

"One of these evenings, my love, I shall not be so easy to get rid of." She held him by the arm.

"Soon, Robert. Very soon."

One of the girls escorted him through the house, he was not sure which of the girls was which; while the other, rescued Rebecca from herself, and from him.

A promised outing.

As Robert approached the house the next evening, ready to go over the garden wall as had been agreed upon, he was met by James, even as he passed the driveway.

"Good evening, Robert!" He indicated that Robert should follow him to the house.

"Mrs. Deming and the twins are out of the house, as we had expected, so you shall come in, the regular way. No one of our neighbors can see you tonight, as dark as it soon will be, to provoke innocent, though dangerous questions, though that is unlikely anyway. They are well aware of Mrs. Deming's moods with both her servants, and her children."

James looked up the street into the fading light, but saw no sign of the coach along the street, which was just as well. It would presumably be around the corner and waiting for them, and would not be out of place.

James led the way from the street, and up the long, tree-lined driveway to the house.

He noticed that Robert had the heavy cloak that he said he would bring, over his arm, and carried his stick in his other hand. He did not seem to need to use it to help himself, but then, it was not a walking stick, but had a much more sinister purpose. Hidden within its wooden shaft, was a thin, steel blade that he knew that the young man knew how to use with great effect.

James also noticed that Robert seemed to have a slightly heavier item in his coat pocket too, and that, was undoubtedly the small pistol that he always seemed to carry with him.

James did not like either swords, or guns, but accepted that sometimes they were a necessary part of a gentleman's accoutrements in this life, especially if one had to move about the city on foot after dark. The predations of footpads was becoming more notable, even in some of the better neighborhoods, and burglaries were not uncommon either.

As they entered the hallway, Robert noticed that both Mr. Deming and Rebecca were waiting for him.

Mr. Deming had spoken for some time with Robert the previous night before Robert had left the house. Had Rebecca overheard that conversation and all that had been said about her and plans for her safety and her future, she would have been surprised.

Her father's conversation, and enquiries, had pulled no punches where his daughter might be concerned, nor had he evaded some generally tender subject areas where parents with nubile daughters would be expected to have a protective attitude, but the situation presented to him was also unusual, and he was prepared to overturn a few conventions of his own, when it involved the safety of his eldest daughter.

Robert had been equally candid in his answers, surprising both James, and Rebecca's father, and giving them much more to think about and to discuss after he had gone.

Things were moving far too fast for them to easily comprehend, and they were being moved by this young man, and his own daughter.

Everyone in the house knew that Rebecca was considerably more vulnerable than other young women. Mr. Deming was intent on ensuring that if he passed her into another man's protection—even temporarily—and unthinkable up until now, that he wanted to be sure that her best interests would always be protected. However, he was still not at all easy with what he was learning and had heard about Mr. Hannan. There were matters of trust, and of being faced with choosing from the lesser of many evils, while hoping that nothing went wrong for his vulnerable daughter.

They always had to try and remain one step ahead of Mrs. Deming. As long as they were able to do that, they might outwit her, and succeed, before she had time to discover what was going on.

Robert's heart had been singing, his step was light, and his mind busy as he had walked home that night. It was fortunate for him—but perhaps for them, too— that no one decided to accost him on his stroll through the poorly lit streets to get back to his own home, which was already in process of being changed, with other plans that he was prepared to bring into effect on short notice.

Sometimes the dark streets were too dark for the villains to be comfortable too, if they could not gauge the nature of their victim.

A sober gentleman carrying a stick, but not using it for walking, provided enough warning. Especially as he gave every appearance of being sober, and was not approaching from the direction of the City and its numerous, 'gentleman's clubs'.

The Watch had also been too attentive of late, to those not dressed as gentleman.

Later the next morning, Mr. Deming had an extensive talk with his daughter, to confirm much of what he had learned from Robert, and to learn from her, what she thought, and might know of this strangely serious young man. He had trod carefully, and cautiously, trying to find out what her feelings were for Robert, though he had seen enough to know what her feelings had been that previous evening.

He was concerned to realize that she seemed to know far more about Robert than he did. She had learned everything James knew; insisting on being told every detail, every gossiped tale and its likely veracity, as well as finding out what her brother knew of him.

Rebecca may, in truth, know more than he did about that young man!

She had not been afraid to voice her innermost thoughts or her delicate feelings, openly, to her father. He—as well as her sisters—had been her confidant for as long as any of them could remember, and she hid little from any of them, except now she did have secrets that she was reluctant to share, but that time was also overdue.

Her father had been concerned at what he heard so openly expressed when he sat down with Rebecca and they'd spoken candidly to each other; though he recognized that this moment must come to most parents, and that it would always be unexpected and unwelcome, for the most part.

His daughter had come of age some time before, and he had not noticed it. He had thought she was still his little girl, and still needed his protection; which she had, but not anymore. Someone else, a relative stranger, was taking over that role.

He was suddenly brought to realize, that if his daughter were to have her way, and she undoubtedly would, that that role would soon need to be voluntarily relinquished, or it would be decisively taken out of his hands by them both. It made him both sad, and relieved, yet it merely replaced one worry with another, and very different one.

Rebecca greeted Robert by reaching out to him, feeling him touch her hands, kiss them, and then to bring her into his arms to embrace her, heedless of her father standing there, and learning of these obvious feelings that these two shared.

Her father hoped that Rebecca's senses, and the absence of that most important one, had not rushed her along too far, or too fast, in her trust of someone she really did not know. He gradually began to believe that their feelings for each other were genuinely felt, and that they knew far more about each other than he wanted to know.

In his questioning of Robert, the evening before. He had not liked all that he had heard; but that, is the nature of an honest and open conversation. The truth can often be hurtful and unpleasant, and Robert had hidden nothing from him, he was sure of that.

He had heard much more than he had been aware of, but as most of it might be easily verified, and certainly did not paint quite as bad a picture as it had, when the gossips had moved it around, he accepted that he had heard the truth on this occasion from the man, himself.

They watched, as Robert wrapped the heavy cloak about Rebecca's shoulders, tied it, and raised the hood over her head.

She felt at the neck of it and discovered a cameo broach sitting on it that must have belonged to Robert's mother.

He had not known it was there, and it brought back tender memories. Her delicate fingers traced out the image upon it.

"It is yours, my dear, if you will accept it?"

"Papa?" She still needed her father's permission for that.

"Wear it, my dear. It may distract a little, from other scrutiny." He kept his other concerns to himself.

She could have been a monk in his cloak and cowl, unrecognizable in the shade it provided to cover all of her identity from a casual glance, and even from one, more focused.

What gave the lie to any of that, however, were his daughter's white and delicate hands, and her feet and shoes, seen fleetingly beneath the long cloak as she moved.

Robert turned to Mr. Deming.

"We shall be back in about an hour and a half, Sir; two hours at the most. We shall leave my carriage at the end of the street, where it is now, and walk from there."

"We'll be watching for you anxiously, Robert."

That, was an understatement.

"I doubt we will be at ease until we see you return!

"If one of us was to go with you, which James and I discussed, our presence might attract the wrong attention to the pair of you."

He put his hand on Robert's arm.

"Do not be any longer than two hours if you can avoid it, or there may be difficulty in other directions."

Robert knew what her father meant.

Mrs. Deming was expected back by then, if her schedule had been adhered to. If not, she might be home earlier. No-one could be sure that she would adhere to it, but if the worst came to the worst, they could always enter the house by the other way.

'Or...' but Robert had not discussed that possibility with them. He would soon need to raise it.

They watched the pair of them walk arm in arm down the driveway and turn up the street.

It would be a long and anxious two hours for them.

The Recital.

Once in his carriage, they settled back onto the cushions, holding hands as they headed for the promised recital in his late father's coach. Rebecca's excitement at going out at last with Robert, was palpable.

She could not trust herself to speak, just happy to have Robert describe everything to her as they moved, drawing ever closer to the cathedral.

Robert kept up a gentle running commentary as they passed through the darkened streets at a sedate and safe pace. The press of people increased as they drew closer to the Cathedral, and there were more carriages, but it seemed to attract more persons on foot, from the local area, than it did of those who drove there.

At the street selected for their drop-off, Dawkins; the coachman, pulled the horses to a standstill and saw his passengers alight.

"In one hour, Dawkins. Here. Though we may be a little longer than one hour."

"Aye, sir. But safer for me to wait for you, than you, waiting for me. I have an obvious blunderbuss and my pistols for trouble, and I even have my old saber by my leg too, whereas you have but that little popgun of yours, and that murderous piece of steel. I know about these areas all too well."

Together, Robert and Rebecca walked back a little way to join the main street, leading them to the Cathedral, which was just visible; visible to Robert anyway, projecting high above the surrounding roofs of houses, most of which were belching thick smoke as the evening grew colder. Robert continued to describe everything he could see as he held Rebecca securely, her arm tucked into his to stop them being separated with them being repeatedly jostled.

The crowd grew thicker as they approached the steps.

"Ten steps up, my love, and then a narrow entrance which I will guide you through."

At the top, he pulled her closer to him, with both hands on her waist, him behind her, at the top, as the throng had to squeeze through the relatively narrow doorway, before it opened out into the cavernous space in which even the faintest of sounds, echoed eerily about. The sudden, sharply amplified noise of boots on the paving stones within the cathedral made more noise than most were comfortable with.

Voices, suddenly dropped in awe and out of respect.

"We shall sit in the pews near the back, where we will attract the least attention, and can leave without attracting any obvious notice. In any case, the light is poor, as I thought, so I doubt we will be much noticed in this crowd."

They sat, as the main part of the Cathedral in front of them proceeded to fill. The organist was well known, and had attracted a large crowd of worshipful listeners, many of whom had never experienced anything like this before.

As the appointed hour drew close, the noise gradually subsided as the crowd fell silent.

The doors closed, echoing along those hallowed spaces, dissuading all late-comers, and warning them that a recital was now in progress.

Eventually, one might have heard a pin drop. Robert knew where to look for the organist, and noted a small figure, dwarfed by most of the individual organ pipes; some, thicker than a man and ten times as tall, which extended far off to each side of him and before which he sat, in the large space up above everything. He saw the organist take his place.

Robert had his head close in to Rebecca, keeping his voice low, and then, as others glared at him for daring to speak at this time, he became silent.

There was the faint 'wheezing' sound of the organ bellows being worked somewhere close by the organ. It might take a small army of men to provide enough wind to give full voice to all of those pipes.

Robert squeezed Rebecca's hand, leaned into her, and warned her in a low voice, that only she might hear this time, that it was about to begin and not to be too startled. He could see her profile, and could not resist kissing her on her cheek before he moved away from her.

At that moment, the organ blasted into voice with the opening notes of Bach's Toccata and Fugue, to reverberate around the large space, before pausing; then picking up again.

That such a diminutive figure, sitting before that wondrous beast, could give rise to such magnificent tones, was enough to overawe anyone, and everyone.

The audience was stricken immobile in sudden surprise and rapt admiration. They probably wondered, as Robert did, how such a gifted artist might appear in their society? How had he acquired such skill and artistry? Yet there were many such men in different courts throughout Europe; in the churches, and all of them in service of sovereign, as well as the church.

Robert felt Rebecca's hand tighten in sudden surprise and awe, at the sheer, overpowering majesty of it all. He looked at her and saw only her hood as she had her head bent forward, so that she could concentrate, while presenting nothing of her face for anyone else to see.

She had hold of the broach on the cloak, with her other hand, as though afraid to lose touch of the first present that Robert had given her, apart from that first kiss, as the reverberating tones occupied her senses.

He felt her trembling with uncontrollable emotion beside him, and comforted her by holding her hand in both of his.

He understood how she felt. She could even be crying. He was close to it himself, feeling the same emotions that she felt.

She, was luckier than any of those others here. Robert knew that she would be able to replay the music as she heard it, over and over in her head, as she undoubtedly would all night, to relive the experience. It was a sound, once heard and experienced, that would never fade from one's mind.

There were a few latecomers, but they were careful to walk as silently as they could, to find an empty space in the pews toward the back with them, and to disturb as few people as possible.

The Toccata and Fugue was followed by less thunderous, though no less magnificent pieces, and then gave way to the more gentle music of Handel.

As the music unfolded, he recalled his grandfather relating how he had been in a small church one Sunday in the city, when the great Handel himself had appeared, and requested to play the organ, to play the guests out of the church after the sermon.

His grandfather had been in awe, as he told how those who had just left, or were leaving the church, were so entranced by the skillful playing emanating from the church organ, that they immediately returned inside, with others following them off the street, until the church was packed more fully than it had been for the sermon, and there was room only for others to stand.

It took over an hour, so his grandfather said, before the reverend had dared to suggest to Mr. Handel, that as long as he played, no-one would be likely to leave the church that day, and that perhaps, please, might he stop playing to let his parishioners go to their homes, to their needed rest!

Robert would relate that memory to Rebecca, but not at this moment. He would leave her with the grandeur of it all reverberating through her mind, and not interrupt anything, with his relatively mindless chatter after her hearing that magnificence.

Seen and Recognized.

To Robert's surprise, he became aware of one other looking at him and his companion from along the same row in which they were sitting.

He recognized one of Rebecca's sisters. She leaned to her twin, to tell her of what she had seen, no doubt aware, that the hooded figure with Robert had to be their sister. Their father had not said that Robert would be taking her to the concert. The less they knew, the safer it would be for Rebecca, even though they would never have told their mother anything.

Robert was able to also see their mother for the first time. He was astonished beyond belief.

She was the image of Rebecca herself, though older, of course. Still, they could have been mistaken for sisters, from what little he could see of her.

He sat back, shocked, but knew he had been seen by the girls. He hoped they would say nothing to their mother. Not that it mattered.

Mrs. Deming's hair, her features in profile; her build; everything about her, was her daughter, Rebecca.

He would need to think extensively about what that meant, though he could see why their mother might be horrified to think that Rebecca, had she gone out into the city, might be confused with her.

Both girls quickly glanced at them, smiling, and then sat back, in order not to draw their mother's attention to what they had seen.

The girls did not pay them any further attention after that first glance, or draw the attention of their mother to him. She wouldn't have known who he was anyway. They had never met or been introduced. Robert decided he would say nothing of it to Rebecca to make her nervous, but would let her focus upon the music.

Rebecca had enough to fill her mind with the music and did not need any distraction to upset her peace, for all the good it might achieve. It would not achieve anything but in an awkward and upsetting way. Better if she were not aware of it. He found that he suddenly had much to think about and to try and understand about Mrs. Deming whom he had only known from her voice.

Once the recital had drawn to a close, Robert had to draw his companion to her feet--she was still lost in the music--and put his arm about her pulling the cloak, close around her, as they left down the wide central aisle and hopefully would get home before the others.

Rebecca seemed to be struck utterly speechless as she walked beside him in her own dream world with her arm threaded through his. He had known she probably would be totally lost in her emotions after that experience, but would not have denied her the experience for the world, and did not break too obviously into her thoughts, letting her come down from the uplifting experience in her own way.

As they left, he noticed that Rebecca's sisters were ensuring that they did not leave quite so quickly from the other end of the pew. It appeared that one of them; hard to tell which one, had lost her glove, and insisted on finding it before they could leave, much to their mother's impatience and aggravation.

He would thank them both later.

After they'd joined the carriage again, exactly where they'd left it, and had ridden it in complete silence to alight near her home, he dismissed the coachman, telling him that he would walk home alone, later.

They walked as quickly as they could down the street, meeting James as expected in the gate.

"The others did not arrive yet, did they, James?"

"No, Robert."

"Good, then they are still behind us, but not far. They were also in the Cathedral and attending the same recital, though they got in late."

He was aware that Rebecca had started beside him on hearing that.

"Only the twins saw us and recognized me, and they tried to ensure that we would have time to arrive back here before they did. Please thank them for us, if I cannot."

James noticed that Rebecca was silent, almost as though struck dumb by what she'd heard of the music, with it still churning around in her mind. She had known she could not possibly be recognized, and almost did not care, considering what she had just heard. He wished he had been there to experience it himself.

He hustled them deeper into the house and up to the top floor, ignoring the complaints from the floorboards in that one section of the corridor.

They were able to hear a coach turning into the stable yard behind the house, as the others returned.

Once onto the top floor and out of the way, Robert laid his cane down inside the door, and removed Rebecca's cloak before he guided her over to sit in her chair.

He had been right. She was still dazed at the experience, and her cheeks were still moist from the tears she had shed. Robert sat opposite her and smiled, as he reached over and held her hands.

"Oh, Robert!" She found her voice at last. "That was magnificent! When might we go again? I will never hear enough of that! What did I just listen to? How can such a large sound come from any instrument?"

"It is a very large instrument my dear, that would fill this entire room twice over and is twice as high. The thickest pipes are the girth of a man or more and as tall as this house, and the smallest are like the stems of your roses but without the thorns. The organist, and those who provide wind to the pipes by working the bellows for the musical 'voices', have to work extremely hard, but especially the organist. In the Tocatta and Fugue-- the first piece you heard, by Bach-- the section where there was only the lowest, thunderous tones, some two minutes into the piece, but for just a few seconds, were from the pedals beneath his feet, and came from the largest of those pipes. A good organist uses hands and feet through-out to achieve the music."

"No wonder he only played for an hour! He must be exhausted." She sat back.

"Oh, my head is filled with the music still! How will I be able to sleep after that?"

Such Excitement

"Rebecca!" The twins came silently into the room, but also in great excitement, bubbling with emotion.

"You were there! How brave of you! We recognized Robert, and knew immediately who the mysterious, hooded-lady with him had to be.

"We had not planned to go to the concert, but we were in the vicinity of the Cathedral and heard the sounds of the organ just beginning and could not leave. We persuaded Mama, that we should go in and listen!

"If we had known you might be there, we would not have done any such thing, of course. Mama was quiet the entire time; unusual for her. We expected her to complain about the noise and that she was getting a headache, but she didn't.

"After it was ended, we tried to give you enough time to arrive back before we did, and I see that we did. Mama grumbled the whole way home and took herself off to bed complaining that she was getting a headache; not wishing to admit that she had enjoyed listening to the music, so that is why we were able to come up so quickly as we did."

They realised that they had interrupted and intruded into a delicate situation, and that they had gone on, for too long. Their eyes met, both having the same thought.

"However, we have not eaten, and I can see that you wish to be alone, so we shall leave you two, go and refresh ourselves, and make up for the meals we missed.

"We had an exhausting day. Mama is so unimaginative, and can be very wearing, but you already know that. However, we are giving you warning that we may come and see you later, if we may, and tell you all that we did. Or perhaps not!"

"Of course, you should come. We will always welcome you, won't we, Robert?"

"Always."

She squeezed his hand for answering as he did, even though it would interrupt them, though never in an unpleasant way.

"When you come, we can discuss what we all just heard. How I ache to try and play that upon the harpsichord."

They each kissed Rebecca, while looking approvingly at Robert for what he had dared to do, taking their sister to that performance. One of them even took his hand by way of thanks and leaned over to kiss him on the cheek. She stood up from him, and mouthed the words, 'thank you' to him, before her sister took her hand and left with her.

"How do you know which sister is which?" It was a natural question concerning twins.

"How would I not know? We grew up together and have always been close. How would I not be able to tell my own sisters apart? But Robert, enough of other things. I wish to relax with you, to feel you holding me, and to hear that music still playing in my head."

Another thought suddenly broke into her consideration.

"Robert?" He waited to find out what she would ask. "When can we go out again? I like being out with you. I like being everywhere and anywhere with you."

He smiled and also chuckled.

"As I do with you, my love. I was giving thought to that, even as we were driving back, but I will have to clear it with James and your father first. Tell me, what time does the house usually stir itself in the morning?"

She liked the way this was going.

"The servants are up by six, but my sisters, generally do not stir until nine, or later, and Mama is rarely up before noon."

"Then we should be able to enjoy any morning to ourselves with much less likelihood of detection, and probably more privacy than in the evening. You will need my cloak if we are to do any of that, so I will leave it with you, if you can hide it safely away somewhere."

She stood and took his hand.

"Come, Robert, I will show you."

She led him across to the door, through it, and into the dark corridor beyond, leading him across to a door on the other side which led into another dark attic room above another part of the house.

"Mama will not hear us. She sleeps on the lowest floor."

Robert could see nothing in the dark, relying upon her knowledge of what lay beyond the door to protect him.

He felt her close the door behind them, take his hand, moving to one side, and showed him, by touch, in the dark, a row of pegs, high on the wall to the left, and behind the door. He felt other clothing already hanging there.

"This is where I keep a change of clothing, and towels for when I get wet in the garden. Mama dare not come in here, either in the dark or at any other time. It is used mostly for storage. We tell her that there are bats in here, and that keeps her out, but if there are any, they are flying around outside by now." She continued to explain.

"We can hang your cloak on that third peg from the right. It is empty."

She felt him feel for that peg and hang the cloak there. Her hand encountered his, as she reached out, checking that the broach was where she remembered it.

It would be safe from her mother, here.

As he turned from doing that, he felt her come closer to him; feeling her arms go about his neck and pull his head down to her for a kiss. She moved even closer into him, kissing him almost ferociously for some time, holding him to not let him escape.

"James will not come in here." She explained that, so that he might be able to relax better.

She felt along his arm and took his hand, raising it to her lips and then snuggled into it, encouraging him to caress her face, which he did.

"Thank you for this evening, Robert, though I doubt I will ever be able to thank you enough."

"It was my pleasure. You are so easy to please."

"I wondered what there was that I could do, that could possibly give you as much pleasure as I was feeling, and I hit upon a way. However, I confess that in my utter selfishness, I know that it will probably give me just as much pleasure, if not more, than I know it will give you."

One surprise after another.

He felt her doing something to her dress, and then heard it rustle to the floor around her ankles. If that was what he was hearing, it was all the more tormenting that he could not see, what she had done. He so much wanted to see her body, and the expression on her face. But he could do the next best thing, and touch.

She took his hand again and raised it to sit full upon her exposed breast, feeling him tremble, hearing his breathing change.

His other hand dropped behind her, feeling that she was indeed entirely naked now, and he gently held her, upon her soft cheek as she moved closer into him. She felt his hand move even further behind her, and his fingers begin to explore and touch her between her legs from that direction, feeling that same hair that he had touched that previous evening, as he moved it aside from getting between her labia, and out of his way.

She relaxed into him with a sigh, feeling his kisses, as well as his building excitement for her as she moved her legs apart to help him discover so much more about her, as he had begun to do that previous evening.

She would never get enough of this feeling.

He kissed all over her shoulders, upon her breasts, and then came back to her lips. They were both breathing hard in their excitement.

"Robert!" Something had disturbed her. Had he hurt her? Had he been too eager?

He tore his mind back to where it should be, not sure if he could stop, though he knew that he had to.

"Yes, my love." He was beginning to perspire and his breathing was becoming labored.

"I hear James setting the table for us. Damn! Oh dear. I did not want this to stop. I know it is not fair upon you, Robert." She touched him there, feeling his excitement for her already, bringing him back down to earth.

She had almost undone his clothing; had got a start on it. If she had done that and found out about him, he could not have stopped.

Everything that was happening, left him breathless. She had shown no restraint. He heard her chuckle mischievously in front of him as she began to refasten his clothing, having some difficulty until he helped her, guiding her hand to refasten some buttons that neither of them could see. She would surely know all about him from the pressure she could feel against her fingers as she fumbled with him there.

She waited for him to help her in turn, intending to do nothing for herself knowing how everything about her excited him, and not wanting to deny him any of it. He would be unable not to touch her everywhere, as he helped her.

"We shall do better, later, Robert."

With that promise, anything would be possible.

He felt her hand on his head as he dropped to his knees slowly, in front of her, kissing her breasts, then her naval on the way down, kneeling in front of her, sliding his hands down her body; her back, her side, over her cheeks; kissing her upon that small patch of hair; nudging her legs apart to kiss her much more personally even than that.

She helped him find out so much more about her, and how moist she had become for him, pausing only while she held him there, where she wanted him to be, and breathing more noticeably herself with what he was doing as he picked up her dress from where it was resting on the floor. He lifted her foot and moved it back, so that she stood within the circle of her dress before he could raise it upon her, but not wanting to hide anything—not from his sight, as he could see nothing—but from his suddenly vibrant senses. He raised it upon her; hesitating, as he got to certain places, pausing at her breasts, kissing them again, letting her dress fall as he found out about them again, then had to begin over. She chuckled at his helplessness when confronted by her naked body.

As he fastened the top buttons on her dress, kissing her, she asked a question that she already knew the answer to; the safest kind of question.

"Robert? Does it give you as much pleasure as it gives me when you touch me and kiss me there?"

"At least as much pleasure, my love. You are slowly driving me insane with desire."

"I think I know how that feels, Robert, but I am not sure if anything could ever exceed the way I already feel. Yet I sense that there are other things we have not yet done, that might exceed that, if I understand my own feelings, but I am ignorant of these things and my sisters cannot, or will not tell me."

"You are correct. There are other things yet to discover, my love about this relationship between a man and a woman who are in love."

She had made a start on learning about one of those things, but then James had intruded by making a noise, setting their table for a late repast.

"But here, and now, is not the place, Rebecca. We need to be alone for a good length of time, and be sure of not being disturbed. Somewhere very private."

She sighed. She knew of such a place, but would not suggest it just yet.

"James will soon return with our meal, Robert, so we should not be away from that room for too long, or he will check in the garden. However, before we leave, Robert'--she hesitated--" what I did, was to try and thank you for a truly memorable evening, and a most wonderful present, which I shall treasure forever. I wanted to make sure that you had something equally memorable of me, but we didn't have time, did we?"

He would not argue. He would remember this moment for the rest of his life too.

"Now, Sir. Robert. Before we forget ourselves again, and I throw other temptations in your way while I am so sorely tempted, and while we are alone, we should go and eat, before James comes looking for us."

She took his hand and led him back across the corridor, carefully closing the door behind them and making sure it was latched.

"Before we eat, or after, you shall clear it with James about us walking, early in the morning, but I know that after this evening, they will not refuse us, now that they know how it can be done, and that you are to be trusted."

He stopped her. "But, Rebecca, surely you know by now, after that, that I am not to be trusted."

"How so, Robert? Everything that just happened was, me. I decided that it would happen so I would say that you cannot trust me to behave as a lady should. Furthermore. I don't care. I am in love. Nothing should be allowed to come between us."

He was also in love.

"I shall resist telling the twins about our plans, or they are likely to want to join us in the morning as we go for a walk, and I want you all to myself."

She opened the attic door, able to smell the additional candles that James had lit for them before he'd set the table.

"After we have eaten, if you do not mind, Robert, when my sisters join us, as they undoubtedly will, I must allow you to leave us, so that I may retire early, for once, if I can, if they will let me, and rest, with my many thoughts and strange emotions. But I shall expect you by first light in the morning, or just before, so that we will not be seen leaving the house, if you can manage that…." Her voice changed.

"Though you may be rethinking the desirability of knowing, such a forward baggage as I become around you. You may not want to come, if I have frightened you off, by my being so demonstratively forward with you, and so shamelessly bold."

He kissed her. "I thought I was the one being too bold; you merely started it when your dress accidentally fell to your ankles." She hit him playfully on the arm. There had been nothing accidental about it and he knew it.

"Then I shall be ready to go out with you then, if you dare to come."

He could not immediately leave her but stayed for another kiss, this time much more gently, and for longer. He felt her move even closer to him, unafraid by what she could feel of his excitement for her, and felt her breathing become more labored. She even seemed to sob and to melt further into his arms, ready to give up everything to have him stay, and to never leave her.

He nuzzled into her hair and kissed her on the neck, and then gently nibbled at her ear.

"I think that answers your question, Rebecca. If I may want to come indeed! Such thoughts! I doubt that an army could keep me away from you at this moment."

She was happy with that response, knowing that she had not frightened him away from her.

"If you say such nice things and return my kisses and my… affection, as you did, Robert. As we did, and you touch me, caress me, touch me so boldly as you did between my legs, and do not leave while you can, you may never get out of here. I will be unable to let you go. I may have to beg James to restrain you and carry you to my lair."

Robert had the same feelings. "I know how we both feel! I would be unable to leave. But I find that I would not mind that fate either. Not for myself! But I must still think of protecting you from me."

"Pooh! You have that the wrong way around, Robert."

She hugged him close. "Be careful. I am very dangerous for you. More dangerous by far than you might know. I am Circe!"

He chuckled.

"You think you are dangerous for me, Rebecca, but you are not. You took the very words out of my own mouth. We appear to be dangerous for each other. I am not sure I will survive being away from you for even a few hours. You will not be safe with me if you encourage me in this way. But I should prefer it if you do not turn me into a pig just yet, not until after we have made love properly, but if you do, then I could live in your garden."

She found that thought, funny, and wanted to know what he meant by, 'make love properly'.

"We must dine now, Robert, and then you shall leave. If you delay too long, we will both be completely lost, and you will never leave, as I will not let you!"

Oh, the promise contained within that statement!

He found he would not mind that fate, but she might, if she thought about it. Everything would change, and be changed for her in ways she might not understand or recognize…or welcome. A man was a strangely demanding beast, full of unbridled passion once he was given his head.

"Oh, what am I thinking, and daring to say?" She was surprising even herself.

"I shall console myself that you will return first thing in the morning, Robert, and I shall be ready to go with you then."

Yes. One step at a time, and not rush anything! But they were only words and thoughts. The reality was staring him too obviously in the face. With her, and after what she had dared to do, and had even begun upon with him, there would be no such thing as one step at a time, or not rushing anything!

She had given him life again. He was living. He was alive, and he was loved and, more important, he was in love.

Adventures. Walking and Climbing, Trees.

Early the next morning, while it was still fairly dark, and before anyone else was abroad, Robert returned to the house, and clambered up the tree and over the wall, learning how easy it was.

He saw no one moving in, or around the house, but there was already fresh smoke billowing from one of the chimneys, so someone was up.

He followed that same directions that Rebecca had taught him to open that secret door into the garden, and climbed slowly up the stairs to the attic, cautiously feeling his way, to stand on that small landing at the top, in the dark.

He fumbled for the latch, and slowly opened the way into the upper room. He could not see Rebecca at first, but he was left in no doubt that she was there and waiting for him. As he regained his feet, he felt her rush over to hold him and kiss him warmly.

He was happy to be greeted that way, even though she almost bowled him off his feet.

He returned her affection for some moments as he pulled her into him, resting his head into the crook of her neck, then kissing each other. Eventually, they broke away from each other.

"That greeting, *almost* begins to make up for the emptiness I felt when you so cruelly banished me from your presence last night, after all of that promise."

"I did not banish you, Robert! I would have preferred you to stay, as dangerous for you as that would have been!"

She blushed. "Oh dear, I am letting my emotions run away with me at what is suddenly happening to me, and I am being too forward again. I was trying to protect you from an intent and shameless hussy. Me! But obviously, in the way I greeted you, I am failing even before I begin, and my sisters will not be pried from their beds before nine or even ten o-clock in the morning to protect you!"

It was interesting for him to hear her saying that she was the dangerous one for him.

She led him out of the room and down the dark stairs, into the main part of the house. Robert carried his boots and his stick in his other hand. She was already wearing his cloak with the broach sitting upon it. She had been waiting for him and wearing it, as she'd waited in anticipation of his arrival.

They were careful to avoid the noisy section of floor, though she doubted that her mother would hear it anyway. Her bedroom was some distance from that part of the house.

"I told James what we planned, and he will let us out. There is no-one else, and very few servants about, this early, and he will leave the main door unlocked so that we may return the same way.

"He said that you must check at the bottom of the driveway when we return. If Mama is unexpectedly moving about, he will tie a piece of ribbon where you can see it on the gate, as a warning not to come in this way, but to come in the other way, and to hope that no one sees us climb the wall. I am not sure how I will manage to maneuver that tree if we do need to go that way."

"I will see to you getting over it. I am not such a weakling that I cannot lift you into that tree, but you will have to hold on tightly, where, and as I tell you to. I can also easily get you across to the wall and even down into the garden too. My strength is rapidly returning, now that I have a new purpose, and someone worth protecting; even depending upon me to escort her safely about the city."

Once outside the door, he adjusted his cloak about her and put the hood up over her head. He noticed that she had sturdy shoes upon her feet for walking. They looked to be almost new.

"Where are we to go, Robert?" She threaded her arm through his, and they walked toward the city.

"We shall not go far this first time, so that I can see how well you stand up to walking some distance, but we shall stay close to your home. I need to explore this area where you live, and find out what is around us."

He patted her hand.

"I shall talk all of the time and describe what I see. You can interrupt anytime to ask any question you might have. Some other time we may get down as far as the river, though the smell is quite bad at times."

She knew about that. "Shakespeare had a very pointed description of that, and its 'villainous smells'."

"Yes, he did. Is there anything you do not know, Miss Deming?"

"If you call me, Miss Deming, in that censorious kind of way, I shall begin to despair of you, Robert. You will set everything back a few days, and I do not wish to lose any of the ground I have so far won, yet it might be safer if I did."

"Too late for that, my love. There are three things that can never be re-called."

She told him. "Time. A spent arrow. And the spoken word."

"I knew I could rely upon you to know that."

There were other examples that were spoken of, sometimes seriously; sometimes jokingly, from where he had been, on the Peninsula. 'A cannon ball, once fired by accident, and sometimes not by accident. A disastrous battle. Or one's ejaculate into one of the many, eager, camp-followers'. He would soon be able to tell her about that.

He was happy to see that the streets were empty at that time in the morning. They had left early enough that no one would see them leave. At that hour, even those with criminal intent had been in their beds for an hour or more, but Robert still carried his stick with him, and there was the reassuring presence of his pistol, nestling in his pocket, out of sight.

That morning was repeated each day that the weather held fine. Their evenings were spent reading, or just talking, often with her sisters sitting with them, so there was rarely time to explore other parts of their growing relationship that had been promised that night of the concert. Her sisters had expressed no desire to get out of bed as early as Rebecca did, to go for a walk with her and Robert, but were happy to join them both of an evening and learn where they had been and what they had seen.

Robert suspected that either Rebecca herself, or James, or their father, had put them up to joining them, to be sure that things did not get out of hand between them, as they so easily would have done.

They even managed to play various card games with a specially-marked deck of cards that Rebecca could use. Those delightful moments would live with them forever.

It was surprising that their mother did not hear their laughter, and come and investigate, but James and their father were always a few moves ahead of her… a few moves ahead of all of them, as they stood back and watched and listened.

Rebecca wondered aloud what his own servants might think was happening. He spent far more time with her, than he did at his own home, but he laughed it off, telling her that he would take her home with him on one of their outings, and then they would soon understand for themselves why he was out for so long and why he came in so late, and left so early.

As each day went by, he and Rebecca grew even closer together, managing to go even farther afield as her feet hardened, and as her shoes were broken-in.

They seemed to be able to get back early enough in the day to miss both her sisters, and their mother, or were able to join her sisters for breakfast or lunch.

Once; on the fourth such outing, Robert noticed a ribbon tied upon the gate, as they were ready to turn into the driveway. He hesitated, knowing what that meant.

"We need to go in the other way, my dear. James has alerted us to your mother being up and about."

They walked further around the house, to the walled-in garden. There was enough underbrush at the base of the tree, and it was thick enough with leaves, that it was obvious that no-one would see them using it as they now must.

"I hope you are ready for your first lesson in tree-climbing, my love? You need have no fear, I shall not let you fall."

Falling, was not what she feared.

He leaned in and kissed her. They kissed often now, in private, and were much less shy with each other than they might have been, but then they had talked of many things, including some risqué subjects as they had walked together. It had been fortunate indeed that no-one else had been able to overhear them. When Rebecca decided that she needed to know something, she would not be put off for long, and could be forthright and expressive herself on so many very personal things once she found that he could not be easily shocked by anything she might say, or ask, or even do.

"I know you won't allow me to fall, Robert. Will you be above me, or below me?"

"Mostly above you, but I will need to get you started. For that, I will be below you."

"Good, but I can see at least one difficulty with my climbing trees in a dress."

So could he. He chuckled, understanding her natural shyness and concern.

"I shall be the only one to see you, my love. However, I should warn you that I shall strive to make sure that I *do,* see more of you, now that you mention such a delightful possibility, and hopefully, without you holding me in great disregard for wanting to do so. Furthermore, I promise that I will not tell; no matter how shocked or bruised I might be by that wonderful experience!"

"Yes, but you…! What an admission, Robert! Though I would not like to shock you so much, too soon!"

She had already shocked him enough when she had let her dress drop to her ankles on that night of the organ concert, and had let him sense what she was feeling for him.

"I doubt that that is possible now, my love; not after that evening of the concert after we'd hung up your cloak. But touching, and seeing—and I have so ached to see you as you are—are two very different things. I touched, and that was excitement enough for a lifetime. Now, I would so much like to see, and to admire more openly, as well as to touch."

She listened, but dare not respond as she would have liked. She would have to consider how to achieve the rest of what he desired.

"I will try very hard not be shocked, Rebecca. But I think I should warn you further, that if the opportunity is there, I shall make sure that I am beneath you at some crucial moment, and you shall hope that I will not drop you in my surprise, at seeing what Absalon encountered and perhaps even do as he did, when he kissed her there. You do remember your Chaucer, I hope."

He felt her become tense. She remembered very clearly.

"Robert! You wouldn't!"

But she knew that he would!

"Robert, if you throw such embarrassing and revealing possibilities at my head, and I fear that it might be unavoidable if you are not a gentleman, that I am unlikely to climb."

"But my dear, you already know that I am not a gentleman. I have given you much proof of that, so many times as we sat together."

"Robert! You should not joke about such an extremely improper thing. I am sure that you would not like to kiss me there either… though you did, earlier, didn't you, in that storage room? And it was not so very...." She sounded surprised to recall that happening. "Still, I cannot imagine why anyone would want to kiss a woman there!"

"You, are not a man in love, my dear, so it may be hard to understand what motivates a man to do what he does. Why should you not be kissed there? Why should you not be kissed everywhere? Little you know yet, of the ways of lovers, or what drives a man along, it seems, but I will be your teacher if you will let me, just as you shall be mine. We made a good start on all of that."

They walked a few more paces in silence. "I do assure you, my dearest Rebecca, that I would like to kiss you there again, or anywhere else you may allow me to! To kiss you everywhere you will permit me. When someone is in love, as I am with you, there is nothing that is improper, you know? All social boundaries and rules are instantly dissolved between them, and they are answerable only to their own consciences. And I do not have one, except where you are concerned."

He sighed. "I should not have told you that; about having a conscience where you are concerned. Damn!"

She came back at him. "You are trying to make something with salacious and reprehensible undertones, sound excusable, Robert!"

"I am trying to, my love. That, is the non-gentleman in me, and the desperate lover."

She repeated those words—*'desperate lover'*. Wanting to ask what he meant, and, at the same time, afraid he might tell her to break down even more of her almost non-existent boundaries.

"I do not mind admitting that I would like to see, fondle, and kiss every inch of your naked body if I had the chance and time enough, but we have never had the chance, or been left alone for long enough."

She began to get an inkling of what he meant, and would give some thought to that too.

He positioned her beneath the first branch and explained that he would lift her, as she put her arms up above herself to find the branch that she would hang onto, while he lifted her high enough to sit on the lowest branch, which was only about three feet off the ground, so she would be in little danger of him trespassing that way with her, unless she insisted that he do so, which she would be unlikely to do.

He would then get her to stand on that same branch, as he helped her to do so, and to move one leg up to the next branch, no more than a couple of feet away and a little higher, while she moved one hand across, to yet another branch.

A man could easily climb such a well-laid-out tree, but it would be full of danger and embarrassment, for a woman, especially for one who could not see.

When she felt secure, he explained that he would climb above her and lift her under her arms to stand on an even higher branch, while she hung on again, and from there it was only a very small step onto the top of the wall, where he would hold her and assist her to sit down. He would then go down into the garden and have her slide off the wall and to fall into his arms... if she could trust him to catch her, or he would stand on the seat and pull her into his arms, touching her the whole time.

"I will direct and assist you to sit down on top of that wall, with your feet over it on the garden side, and then I will get over, and then see about getting you down from there, and then we can go into the house. That is, unless I see something that I might kiss in the interim, either on the way up, or on the way down, or both! Perhaps I should kiss you there now while you stand on that branch, and get this torment for me, out of the way. Or make it worse. You are at exactly the right height, though the object of my present affectionate intent, is obscured by that all-concealing dress! You would not consider raising it a little for me, would you? Please? I would even help you."

She felt him begin to raise it above her knees as she pressed her legs together, complaining, and began to plead with him.

She protested, unable to let go of the branch she was grasping, to hold her dress down.

"Robert! You…! You…! I hear someone close by!"

He knew better. "There is no-one close by, my love. You are blowing smoke about and trying to avoid your inevitable fate. You should stop tormenting me, and surrender gracefully, or I may have to leave you here, while I sulk."

"You would not do that, Robert. I know you!"

He sighed. "Yes, you know me too well. I could neither leave you here, nor sulk, but I would so much like to kiss you there again."

They traversed the wall, without injury, but with a heightened sense of excitement, and made it across to the house, unseen.

Robert opened the section of wall and saw them both inside before he closed it again. As he turned, in the dark space, expecting that she had gone ahead of him up the stairs, he felt her in his arms once more.

"Robert." She kissed him. "How dared you do what you did? Though you did warn me, didn't you? I fear someone may have heard me." She didn't seem too annoyed with him.

"You took me entirely by surprise, and made me scream, even on the way up, before we even got to the wall! And then after... I was a nervous wreck wondering what you would not dare to do next. You knew I could not move, or I might have fallen!"

"I did take advantage of you, didn't I? Both times going up the tree and then once as I helped you down from that wall. I had warned you what I would do if I saw a temptation, and as I did see it, I kissed! I was as surprised as you were, that my hands had moved up and under your dress to your waist as you slid off the wall into my arms. I could not help it if I decided to kiss you there again."

"Liar!" It was not uttered with any malice or anger, however, but with a gentle tap on his arm.

She still complained. It was what was expected of a reputable young woman.

"You made sure that I was put into the position of you... of you not only seeing everything about me, when you got me to move one leg to that higher branch, quite a little bit higher than the one I was on, and further away, and I had my legs so... far... apart…also as you intended, but you took further advantage of me too. I think you interfered with me!"

He had. "But gently and intriguingly!" She had no difficulty adding that comment to excuse his personal trespass.

He smiled and kissed her. "Yes, I did, didn't I? I admit that I interfered! Your legs were entirely, suitably, and temptingly far apart at that moment. But I did not expect that the opportunity would present itself so well for a second time."

Nor had she.

He explained, though he did not need to. "I bent down to retrieve my stick from the ground, so that I could lay it on the wall top, and climb with you. Then, when I stood up, I noticed that it had gone suddenly very dark, yet I knew that it was not that far advanced an hour.

"Imagine, if you can, how pleased I was to discover where I was, and that my head was underneath... and exactly where I wanted it to be, and facing you! How could I not kiss you?"

He smoothed her hair back from her face, and sighed as he kissed her again.

"You know the rest. You would not have refused me. There you were, tempting me as I had hoped might happen. I was breathless with excitement and entirely helpless. I kissed you as I had said I would. I had to."

"You kissed me twice, while I was in the tree, Robert, where you should not have kissed me, and you lingered too long each time, and... touched! And you chuckled mischievously at what you were doing. I could do nothing about it, and I almost fell!"

"You squirmed so delightfully and made such interesting noises."

She chuckled too. "Did I make interesting noises? I think I screamed. I don't recall."

"You screamed very softly, which I took as encouragement to continue."

"Do all lovers do that, Robert?"

"Only if they are as lucky as I am, my love."

He added to that.

"At least they eventually progress to that, if they are so very fortunate and relaxed with each other as we are. Few of them are so relaxed, but are too often tied up in consideration of being proper! I have no patience with such hypocritical propriety."

"We almost made love the other evening, Robert, in the storage room after that recital. I wanted you to. I was trying to encourage you, which was why I got rid of my dress. I would not have minded. I felt you against me then. You were excited, almost as much as I was, but I dared not speak of it at that moment." Nor try to find out more about him, which she had started to do in her reckless excitement.

"I know! Just as well! You encourage me to be like that, from time to time with you, and deliberately so, as when you kissed me then, very tenderly and so revealingly, and came so very close to me. Very close!"

She had also encouraged him, and helped him to find, and to touch her.

"I spent a sleepless night thinking of what might have been, and regretting what did not happen, but then I recalled that your father had threatened me with violence if I were to harm you; and James had done the same, so I needed to curb my eagerness for you."

He kissed her, and found that his kiss was returned.

"But come, my love, we need to get ourselves up there, or James will come looking for you, and beat me within an inch of my life because of what I just did, if he heard you scream as we climbed that tree and as you came off that wall. I am sure he will take just one look at my face, to know.

"Now what are you doing?"

He felt her moving close by him as he held her still.

"I am taking my shoes off. I prefer to climb these stairs without them, or they will clatter too much and alert the house."

She moved on, ahead of him.

They paused at the top in the dark as they listened, to understand who might be in the room before they entered it.

When she let him know that it was clear, he let them both into that now bright room at the top of the house as he helped her climb ahead of him, his hands under her dress once more, causing her to gasp and to move even faster ahead of him.

She climbed out into the room as he followed her closely, holding an ankle to stop her climbing to her feet and escaping him in her excitement with him tormenting her, and they lay together on the floor. She was on her back, with him above her as they kissed.

She waited to see what he would do, other than just kiss her. The unspoken invitation was there, now that he had her trapped.

"In that tree and after, my love… was my touching you, and my kissing you there, as I did, so every shocking and unwelcome?"

She thought for a moment, analyzing her feelings. "No, Robert. Shocking? Yes. Unwelcome? No."

He kissed her, looking down on her, and slowly touched her again beneath her dress, discovering even more about her as she laid there for him with her legs apart, moving them even farther apart as he touched, feeling him move his hand up farther on her body to hold her breast as he kissed her over what had to be at least two minutes, before moving back down again on her to touch her more intimately, feeling her squirm and gasp beneath him, becoming almost as breathless and as agitated as he was.

Unfortunately, they didn't have time to do anything else, as they both wanted. Others were coming! They could hear movement from deeper in the house, and coming closer. Damn!

Once on their feet after a few more moments of adjustment to their clothing, they went across the corridor together, holding hands, still touching intimately, as the opportunity allowed and hung up the cloak again on its peg, holding each other, not wanting to let the other go.

Robert looked around in the daylight flooding through the far window, and could see that it was indeed a storage room, with many items of furniture, including a harpsichord.

"Robert! Close the door quietly, I hear someone coming up the stairs to the attic."

She listened for a while, still holding him very close to her, trapping his hand under her dress, and then he heard her breathe a sigh of relief.

"It's James!"

He was partially relieved, afraid for a moment, that she would get rid of her dress again. There would have been no escape for either of them if she had.

She leaned into him and kissed him again.

"Thank you for today."

He smiled, relieved to be both forgiven and thanked. "Thank you, my love. I am the one in your debt, and to think I very nearly did not meet you that very first day when I was with George."

It did not bear thinking about. Such thoughts could drive a person mad.

She opened the door, and they moved across the corridor just as James appeared at the top of the stairs, following them into the room.

Robert passed him the ribbon he had untied from the driveway.

"I knew you would see it. Mrs. Deming is going out, even now, so once she has gone, there is nothing to stop you both coming down for breakfast with the twins. I imagine that you worked up an appetite, the pair of you. I see that going out like that for the last few days, has put a glow in your cheeks, Miss!"

It had put a bounce in Robert's step too.

He saw her blushing, and wondered if that was all it was.

There had been more than just a walk, obviously, but that was perhaps to be expected. They were both young and obviously so very much in love with each other.

He envied them. He hoped she would not rush things along too fast, but he began to worry less about that, as he learned more about Robert, but it would be a struggle for the poor man with what she would throw in his way to tempt him. Still, they were getting that under control even then.

"Yes. Everything was wonderful, James."

"How far out did you get this time, Robert?"

"We made it down to the river for the first time, with all of its 'villainous smells'—Shakespeare described it that way"... (he felt Rebecca nudge him. She was the one who had told him that)— "so Rebecca told me..." it had been a necessary recovery... "and then we came back by way of the Cathedral and heard someone practicing on the organ, so we stayed for a while to listen, and then we came straight back. I expect we are a little later than we were before, as we went quite far."

"Just a little later." He paused. "I hear the carriage pulling out now.

"Give me five minutes to be sure she went, and if you hear nothing from me, then come on down for breakfast. Mr. Deming will be there too, and I know he has something for you Robert, and to learn more of what you are planning."

Robert doubted he would be able to tell anyone, all, of what he planned with Rebecca, or she, for him. But would do it, only with her permission and willing assistance, of course!

While the weather remained warm and inviting, they spent little time in the house, or the garden, but continued their ramblings about the city and the river, even getting as far as crossing the bridge on one occasion, as he described every single detail to her on that long walk, but telling her that he was unable to see any remaining heads, still impaled on the pikes, above 'Traitors' Gate', on the far end of it.

A Trespass Welcome, and Long Overdue.

It rained for the next two days so they were not able to go anywhere on those mornings as they'd hoped, nor out into the garden of an evening with everything so wet.

Robert still came in the early morning and had breakfast with them, even after eating before he'd left home, though he came not-so-early on each of those days, but he did stay until the early hours of the next morning.

Neither of them wanted to ever be parted from the other, and it was becoming more difficult for him to leave.

No one said anything about him spending so much time with Rebecca, from early until very late, but it was obvious that something would soon need to be said, and questions asked.

They talked extensively as they learned more of each other, or he read to her from their increasing library of books as they both sat in that one chair, or danced in their bare feet around that room, teaching her various dance steps, as they hummed a tune together, to keep time.

They laughed often, but always with a thought as to who might overhear them, or was approaching where they were. It was always either the twins, or James, and rarely, her father, but they were not being left alone quite as much, or for as long as they would have liked, and never knew who was watching them from the shadows or listening from outside of their door.

With time, familiarity, and a growing trust in each other, as well as growing curiosity and intent, those usual defenses of distance - which had long been discarded even after that first night, when they had shared the same chair and sat closely together—care, about how, one sat with the other; what one might say; or adjustments of dress, as they moved to get comfortable together— all gradually relaxed, and crumbled into the dust of inevitability.

It began to seem and to feel, that they had known each other all of their lives. Others just watched, and wondered.

In such closely supervised surroundings (too much had changed), with James, her sisters, or her father likely to intrude at any time and sit with them, though often, with ample warning of their approach, which seemed to be deliberate on their part, considering the noise they made, Robert was not able take any further, significant or desperately needed liberties with her, as he had in the tree or afterward, as they would both have liked him to do, and as she let him know in many different ways as she tormented him, as a woman often will.

She recognized that she missed such playful and intimate expressions of his love for her, and would not have objected if he'd continued with that discovery process each chance they had, rolling it along where they both wanted it to go

She often thought about… and had begun to feel… an awakening of her own sense of what would unfold between them when she was able to make it happen, or she could encourage him, to do so. Except there was always that time factor, and not knowing when, or who, would walk in on them.

If necessary, she would even be forward herself, and encourage him as far as she dared, giving some thought about how to do that without being too obvious about it. But what did 'being obvious' matter, if that was what it would take; asking him to help her in some personal way that there would be no retreating from; though she was not sure what that way would be.

Or maybe she would just plead with him directly and ask him to touch her, caress her, make love to her. He obviously wanted to.

Robert could be mischievous in his own right, even without encouragement, sometimes taking her off guard when he kissed her upon her neck, or on the top of her breasts, visible and easily accessible in the low top of her dress, causing her to gasp in surprise, before he returned to his reading, leaving her heart thumping, and wondering what he would surprise her with next.

At other times he stood with her in the window, behind her, his arms around her, holding her just under her breasts, leaning into her as he described everything he could see outside while looking down into the front of her dress, lifting her breasts higher, so that he could see more of them.

She knew what he was doing, and began to realize that this was the nature of the human male beast; always curious, intent, adventurous, and even insistent, but in a gentle kind of way where she was concerned, and always considerate of her feelings; never wanting to hurt or shock her. At least, not too much.

She knew that there would also come a time when he would not be stopped, and that time was not far away now. She was woman-enough to sense that, recognizing that she would not stop him, but would encourage him, where, and whenever she could.

She breathlessly awaited the next, seemingly inevitable trespass, much as she'd anticipated him doing as she'd climbed that tree ahead of him, knowing what he would do if the opportunity was presented, but never quite sure when that would be; putting her on tenterhooks, and heightening every emotion because of that tormenting uncertainty. No wonder she had screamed--thankfully in a low voice-- when it had finally happened.

She helped the developing situation between them along, as she could, by dressing in an older dress; one, that was shorter and could even be easily slipped off her shoulders if things went that far, or which gave greater access to her body in other ways, so that he could see more of her, or touch more of her as the opportunity and the mood allowed. All she could do was to throw opportunities and temptations in his way. One time....

They sat together in their own little world and listened to the rain outside.

As they moved together and adjusted their positions to arrive at a mutually comfortable sharing of that one chair as they talked and laughed together, it seemed natural that his hand would touch her lower leg as he helped her adjust her dress; or he moved her dress from being rumpled up under her, or behind her, not concerned that, for those changes, his hand was actually under her dress, progressing to holding her for a few seconds upon her thigh or was resting between her thighs. It was all so gradually done.

She said nothing, so he would say nothing, either.

They both knew what was happening.

At those times, Rebecca was not nearly as protective of her modesty as she should have been. She seemed inattentive as to the state of her dress as they sat, huddled close together, and talked or kissed, or read, with them both, happy just to hold each other close and to kiss.

Sometimes her feet were on the seat in front of her, or she moved them across his legs to rest on the far side of the seat, even resting onto the arm of it as she leaned into him, happy to be where she was, listening to the rain outside hammering on the roof immediately above their heads. She was not always cognizant of where the hem of her dress was; and it was never where it should have been... always too high.

She knew that she stimulated him in so many ways. Her body did that to him, especially when he touched it, and not entirely by accident.

She did not understand his interest in her breasts, or what was under her dress, but accepted it. It was all so strange. But why would he not be curious about her body? It seemed to invite his attention. It was nice to be noticed, and held so close, and touched.

She was curious about him; about that strange part of his that she'd gradually discovered for herself in passing, but had never seen or touched properly, or spoke of, and which she had come so close to, a few times, after they'd hung his cloak up in the storage room, after she had.... Had she actually done that... tried to uncover him there after she'd dropped her dress to the floor?

She had. But she'd been very excited at the time and needed him in a strange way, but he had resisted.

He obviously wanted to see and to touch more of her, so she would not deny him that.

Once, he had touched her under her dress, resting his hand for a few moments upon her in a more obvious way, re-discovering a beginning fold of skin hidden in that hair there, but not well-hidden; the top of her vulva. He had touched her there without going any farther, and had remained there for several minutes, with his finger touching into that groove at the top.

They both ignored that, while not actually ignoring anything, as they continued to open up so much more to discover under her dress, as her legs separated for a moment to reveal a suggestion of more of that hair, in a no-longer-hidden or entirely unknown place between her raised legs, or even letting him see down into the front of her dress, which he took advantage of by blowing gently, opening it up more, letting her know exactly where he was, and what he was thinking about.

Sometimes, they sat in front of the open window so that he had his back to the light, reading to her, as she sat opposite him with her feet on either side of his body; sitting back, listening, opening herself up even better for him to observe her with the brighter light shining in upon her there, under her dress. She no longer cared.

She knew exactly what he was doing and what she was revealing for him and was not afraid to move her dress even more above her knees as she helped him learn more of her both by sight and touch.

She was driving him mad. He wanted to touch, and even to kiss again, but lacked the courage at that moment.

She knew all about it. She intended most of it and would allow the rest to happen as it would.

Once, when they shared the one chair, and as they had adjusted their positions in the relative dark later in the evening, she had taken his hand, and had moved it under her dress to touch her, guiding him, saying nothing, wanting him to touch her.

She sat back and moved her hips forward into his hand, wanting him to touch her even more as they'd adjusted their positions, moving her legs further apart, and with encouraging words.

"Robert, you may touch me more down there, please. I want you to touch me everywhere. Do not hold back. You can even... go farther into me with your fingers. It does not hurt, and it is strangely pleasurable."

She allowed her legs to drift farther apart then too, as she had kissed him, in growing excitement herself, feeling him beginning to investigate her deeper, as she'd requested. She surprised even herself at how far he was able to go into her, but she felt very relaxed.

He touched slowly along her, discovering more of her moistness and of that haunting, fleshy groove, and that moist entrance to her body, hidden among the hairs; not closed to him; wanting him to go back into her again, there. He did.

At that moment, others were heard to be noisily approaching, so the opportunity was abandoned as they hurriedly readjusted their positions, amidst a flurry of excitement and chuckling, and picked up where they had left off reading, as though nothing had happened. They both knew better.

He knew that they must both of them look wild-eyed, and guilty when the twins entered for a few minutes to bring up the newspaper that their father had just finished.

They were smiling and laughing to themselves, nudging each other, knowing that they had come up too quickly without adequate warning (deliberately), as they had been told *not* to do, but had hoped to catch them in some way. They had not been disappointed. It was obvious where this was going between them, even though it would be unthinkable in their society... except... Rebecca was different.

"Is there anything you would like us to get for you, Rebecca, Robert?" They giggled, seeing the difficulties they were both having, trying to cover themselves away and to hide what they had been doing with each other. Blushing, wide-eyed, and wild-eyed. "Just tell us, and we will see that it is brought up." A plateful of mischief, perhaps?

It looked like they already had everything they needed.

They had been sent to spy on them.

After her sisters had departed, to report on them and what they were doing (if they chose, or if they dared), the two of them laughed nervously, joining each other again in one chair, snuggling their heads closer together like two conspirators detected in their plot, kissing gently as they laughed, picking up where they'd left off; moving his hand under her dress again to caress her more boldly now, aware that they would have some period of time to themselves before anyone else came up, but still not time enough for anything more intimate as they were both wanting to happen.

They decided that they must be more careful if they could, and not let such activity get too far out of hand no matter how much they both wanted it to, but she could encourage him to go farther into her with his fingers, each time he touched along her, and he could touch her breasts more, too.

He recognized the wonderful, provocative nature that he had sparked in this otherwise modest and beautiful young woman. He loved her the more for it, and even told her so as they had kissed. It had not harmed. The situation only seemed to improve after that, and the temptations to increase, and to become more obvious and inviting, as he'd hoped they would.

"We shall come to grief one of these times if we do not keep our wits about us. If we are not careful, I will be unable to control myself, and will soon 'come', if you know what that means."

She did not know, and it was difficult to explain to her the way he felt. Nonetheless, he tried. They had at least come that far with each other.

"You know that I am aroused most of the time when I am close to you?"

She nodded. "I think so."

She knew all about that, but a wise woman did not usually directly address that item, or talk about it, unless she really wished to find out about it.

"The reason for that, is…." he fumbled for the words. "That awkward part of mine, wants to go into your body, here."

He touched her, letting just the tip of his finger go into her, and left it there as he talked.

"When it goes into you, here, deeply, as it will when we make love, it begins. Then, when I am deep into you, there is another feeling that builds up for me, in an uncontrollable way, and I ejaculate; I shoot my sperm into you. They spurt out of me, tens of thousands of them in each pulse, when I 'come'. That is the expression for it. Sometimes it happens when I am excited enough, and even without my being in you here, where I should be, and where I so want to be, though I have not ejaculated onto you yet." He'd come close to it, several times.

She would need to learn it for herself when it happened, but he could warn her as it was about to happen.

"I think I understand, Robert." She didn't. It would have to happen for her to truly understand it.

"It is already a difficult enough task for me to holding back from doing that when I get excited with you, as I always am, and we are likely to be caught if we go too far down that road like this and I wet myself and you. I do not think you appreciate how devastating you are for me, and how difficult it is to control myself when I am with you."

He was wrong. She was aware of it, and liked the feeling of power that it gave her. She had noted the change in his condition more than once, and could feel him hard, against her legs in some interesting ways, or had accidentally touched him there, or had noticed him becoming harder there when they had kissed for some extended period of time, as they often did now, as he even gently held her breasts by sliding his hand into the front of her dress, or moved under it, raising it high enough to hold her breasts. She might as well not have had a dress on, at those times.

She was always curious about his body too, and his responses to her. She was no longer afraid to move closer into him, to sense what was happening to his body as they kissed and caressed, but she had not actually touched him there yet, to find out more about him.

She nuzzled into him and gurgled at what she sensed of his mood. "Will you 'come', soon, Robert?" She was already curious to find out about that.

"Perhaps."

She backed away and kissed him as she allowed him to recover his thoughts once more, finding that his hand was then inside of her dress from the bottom, and he had raised it to her breasts where he gently held them and discovered that hard peak surmounting them. She was excited herself, and the breathless feeling excited her even more.

Her dress was up to her waist by then, but she was not struggling to bring it down. A very little movement would take if off her.

She could hear no one. She raised her arms and let him do so, lifting it off her. He put it upon the high back of the chair where it could easily be retrieved and dropped back onto her again if they heard anyone approaching.

He leaned into her then to kiss her breasts and all along her body, causing her to gasp and to squirm with him both kissing her and touching her as he dropped to his knees.

She found the courage to say what she was thinking.

"Robert? Would you like to make love to me now? To put that part of yours into me? To come?"

"Yes, my love, I would like that, but I mustn't."

"Why not? We are so close to it."

"I am afraid that I would hurt you, and we would be moving too fast. Two people usually get to know each other for years before they first make love, and then only after they are married. At least that is how it should be done, though some couples get careless and sometimes they get the order reversed."

As they would!

"I don't think either of us will have patience enough for that; to wait that long, Robert. Look at what we did that first evening, as we sat together and explored each other's features, and what we learned about each other. Then, after that concert, though…that was my doing, when I became so bold, wasn't it? And then as we climbed that tree. Nothing seemed to be moving too fast, to me then, or for you. Look at what we are doing with each other even now, with me naked in front you and daring to ask you to make love to me. I want you to. I could not wait for years, not even months or weeks, or any longer. We do not have the time. I want you to make love to me now, Robert."

"Just as I want to make love to you too, Rebecca. Though I fear that is it already galloping away from us, and it is just a matter of time before it is about to get even more out of hand!"

"When you 'come'?"

"Yes. When I 'come'."

He felt her hand upon his face, as her fingers traced out his mouth and his lips, and he stayed still for her. He enjoyed what he was touching in turn, of other, soft lips, and did not wish to move.

He asked. "What would you like to know, my dear, that you do not know already, or cannot read in that way? I will tell you anything you wish to know. I have no secrets from you now, do I?"

"None sir! Nor I from you, I think!" Not with what he was touching. "But though I can feel your features, and sense your emotions and warmer moods, I cannot yet read your deepest, innermost feelings, except when we kiss or… I feel that other that you cannot control very well, especially when you are touching me down there, as you are at the moment."

"That's not surprising. I have trouble with those myself sometimes. My feelings are pushing me in one direction as you well know. I cannot control that 'other', as you describe it, so easily. You, do."

That surprised her, though it shouldn't have done.

"At the same time, I would not like to scare you, and I am afraid, that I would.

"I am terrified of moving too fast for you, and of offending or hurting you. It is a turbulent and troubling conflict. My brain does not know what to think about any of it, and I must rely upon you guiding me in whichever direction is acceptable to you, my love. I do know a few things, however?"

"What, Robert?"

"I know three things, and so do you." He sighed deeply. "Since I came back from abroad, I have not thought very much at all about that other existence; the battlefield, that threatened to drive me mad. I much prefer the way you are affecting me."

He laughed. "I am sure James must have thought me mad on that first evening when he asked me if I had any 'dishonorable feelings' for you, and caught me scrambling to answer."

She was surprised to hear that, sitting up straighter, but pulling his hand back into her to stop him slipping from her altogether.

"He asked you that?"

"He did."

"And did you!"

"I fell in love with you almost as soon as I saw you, and then fell in love even deeper, the more we talked. I am ashamed to say that I did have those feelings for you then. What man would not have? But I had tried not to think about it at all until he asked."

"Why would you be ashamed to feel that way? It was natural, Robert. I feel that way too, about you. One cannot help one's feelings for someone. I am not ashamed of my feelings for you, or what is happening between us."

He sighed. "I tried to answer him honestly, and did so, clumsily. I sensed that there was something strange happening to me, even then, surprised to find that I had any of those tender feeling left in me, and shocked that they were happening so fast."

She came to his defense at that moment.

"I don't think they could be called, 'dishonorable feelings', Robert! I had feelings about you, too. They seemed to be 'inevitable', with us being so close together, the only man outside of my immediate family I was ever so close to, but none of them ever came so close as you do, and family, is different.

"I think I have liked everything that we have done so far. You have always been gentle and considerate, not rushing anything, or taking too much advantage of me, not even as we climbed in that tree. All of that, was inevitable between two persons in love.

"I would like to learn more about all of these feelings. We have progressed very far in just the last few days, but it is also frustrating, not knowing when anyone will walk in on us, when it is clear what we would both rather be doing with each other. You want to kiss me everywhere and make love to me, and I want you to kiss me everywhere and make love to me too."

I was developing the same feelings for you, Robert, even as we talked that first evening. I would call them progressive; exciting; even necessary! Perhaps even adventurous, or daring, as we sometimes are quite often now. And, inevitable!"

She felt his fingers move to explore her body even more where he was touching. She moved her hips forward bringing her leg up onto the seat to open herself better to his discovery, encouraging him, and providing him more room to do so, as she reached out to find out about him, in turn.

She was not sure how to go about that, until he showed her what to undo and where to go, helping her, feeling her discover him, bringing him more to life as she held him, feeling what he had described to her.

She was suddenly very much wide-awake.

Something this big around, and so long, and so hard could not possibly fit into her body, into that so-small, and tight a place.

She tried to take her mind off that.

"I do not think that there is anything immoral, in honest love and true feelings of love, as I feel, and as I believe you feel too, Robert! I found I wanted to know so much more about you in every way, and we did, even on that first night when we touched each other's faces, and in… many other ways, since then, even some of them… just this evening… as we have become more relaxed with each other, like now."

She gasped at what he was doing to her, touching her along her vulva, distracting her, as he moved even closer to her, and deeper into her.

"You said, you knew three things, Robert. What are the other two things that you know?" She continued to help him learn, and discover more about her as she moved with increasing agitation and excitement with him touching her so intimately.

He paused and told her. "I know that I love you more than anything I have ever known before, Rebecca, and that I want to marry you."

He felt her sudden surprise at hearing that, becoming tense, trapping his fingers for a moment.

"Marriage? I did not expect that from you."

"Marriage?" She seemed confused.

"But… but… Robert, I did not expect so much from you."

He felt her take his other hand and hold it up to her face, and he even felt tears upon it.

It was his turn to be shocked now.

"How could you not expect me not to want to marry you? It is what two persons in love will always want to do, though I know that I am rushing everything along. But I have to, for both of our sakes."

What had she expected? That he would just take advantage of her, seduce her, make love to her, and then abandon her?

That, had never been his intent.

"You seem upset, my love! Am I moving too fast for you? Have I taken too much advantage of you too soon? Is it too large a leap from Absalon, to marriage, in just a few days?" He seemed worried at that thought and removed his hand from caressing her.

She laughed at his comment.

"No, Robert. We have come very close to much greater intimacy with each other than that, and are even closer, now, except for our lack of privacy to do so…. And I dare even talk of it without blushing!" She sounded surprised at her own boldness.

"I am sure every woman dreams of being loved, and of marriage, and children. But why would you wish to marry me, Robert? I am not a whole woman. I do not expect it, despite what is happening between us."

He did not know what to think.

"You should not feel that you are obliged to marry me, Robert, even if we do make love, as we soon must.

"I made up my mind, that with you, I will grasp this one opportunity while I can, and experience all that I may of life, before it is lost to me, leaving me with memories to last me for the rest of... the rest of my life, and when you... when you...."

She could not say it; *grow tired of me'.*

"And then you will find a proper wife as befits a healthy young man."

He was struck speechless and could only listen.

"Although, I think I would be privileged, and would become resigned to being your mistress…nothing more than that... if you would have me that way… if you find it as difficult as I would, to let you go.

"I think it is often done, by many men who are not happily married." She thought about that. "Though I do not think that my father has a mistress. I don't think he will ever give up on my mother that way."

He was shocked to hear everything she was saying, what she was inviting from him.

She sighed and continued.

"How dare I think, or admit to that? And yet I do! I thought about it that first night after you had fallen asleep and before James send me to my bed. I would settle for that, if there is no other way!"

Robert let her ramble on, wanting her to tell him everything she was feeling.

"I am blind. and not a complete person – I think that is why my mother hates me. I have no future in that way. I am entirely helpless and cannot fend for myself, and I will be forever dependent upon someone else throughout my life. I would not like to become such a burden upon you and imprison you in that way with me, though, servants…." She left that thought unfinished.

"I needed to find what life, and love had to offer me before that reality intrudes between us. A man needs a healthy wife that might share everything with him, and to raise his children."

The silence extended for too long.

"Please say something, Robert."

He kissed her instead, placing his hand full upon her breast, feeling its smooth, warm, firmness. He had never been so excited for any woman at any time in his life. She came close to him, and his mind became scrambled, barely able to function. Except now, he was thinking very clearly, and was calm, almost angry, when he should not have been. Had he given her this wrong impression of his intentions?

He chose his words carefully. "I want all of that for you too, Rebecca; children also, our children, but you shall not be my mistress.

You shall be my wife. I want you no other way than under the protection of marriage to me, my love, so do not speak so easily of that other, of being my mistress, or of my abandoning you when I grow weary of you, as I will never do that.

"What kind of a man would I be, if I were to toy with you in that way, and not mean it? I would rather cut off my arm, kill myself, than hurt you. I would not be able to look at myself in the mirror after that, so get rid of that notion, my one; my only love."

He felt her trembling with emotion and heard her sob.

He reinforced what he was telling her. "We, you and I, are going to marry. Very soon. You are no more dependent upon others than any other member of our society is. We are all looked-after and waited-upon in one way or another, but you, do so much more than any society lady I ever knew. Some of them refuse to lift even a finger on their own behalf, and demand to be waited upon."

She sensed his aversion to those women

"They, do not deserve marriage. You, do."

He hugged her closer to him and smoothed his hand over her face to wipe the dampness off her cheeks.

"You are much more of a woman, and are more interesting to me than any of them. You are the healthiest and most vibrant woman alive, and one of the most capable that I have come across in a very long time; and the first that has ever interested me in this way that you do. You are not an incomplete person at all, in my view."

She let him speak, needing to hear everything.

"You may have lost one sense, my love, but you more than make up for it with others. You hear, far better than I do. You think clearly, too. You are very intelligent and are widely read, despite your perceived inability. You converse wisely and well, and you are better informed than most others in our society. You are more attuned to subtle emotions, and are able to sense others' feelings, in ways that I will never be able to do."

She was now being quiet as he spoke, needing the hear everything he was telling her. Feeling reassured.

"I do not think that I would choose to be close to anyone else, now that I have met you! I think that you are far more of a woman; vibrant, alive, in every way, more-so than almost any other woman in this city! You laugh easily with me. You are kind, soft spoken, and easy to please. You tolerate my poor reading without criticism, and my occasionally shocking lapses in moral fiber and character when I climb trees with you, kiss you in... in... wondrous places; and work deviously to try to see more of you than I should. Or…, I am so bold as to touch you familiarly, and very intimately! As I am doing now."

He sighed heavily.

"I love you, Rebecca. I can only hope and pray that I deserve your love."

"You do, Robert. You do."

She was bubbling with happiness now, having been reassured that this was not going to end in the worst way for her.

She returned his kiss, took his hand again and directed it more firmly between her legs for him to sense that suddenly moist and warm place; helped to be that way by his kind and wonderful words, and made even-more-welcoming to him, by her sudden, tearful mood of relief, as his hand rested consolingly on that patch of hair between her thighs again as he caressed along her. He sighed heavily, clearly agitated within himself.

"You share my passion for most things, Rebecca; reading, music, walking, and no doubt you will be just as excited when you hear your first orchestra or a string ensemble. We are also learning to dance together. And this!"

He felt her push her thighs forward into his hand to encourage him to touch her more than he had before. She even took hold of his arm and pulled it even harder into her there, demanding he be more aggressive with her.

He responded as she seemed to demand of him, and felt his ears beginning to tingle and his senses to become sharp and intent.

"I am sure you will love to attend an opera or a play, even Shakespeare, where the words are the drama, though we will not mingle with the groundlings.

"I would love to walk along a shore with you, and smell the fresh sea air rather than this choking, charnel smell from the city's fires, or the stench of piggeries, tanneries, and the sickly smell of brewing, and want to feel the sand and pebbles beneath our bare feet, and even paddle there. As long as you are with me."

"And make love in the garden!"

She changed her position again, and helped him move his fingers deeper into that space again, as she opened her legs more for him, moving some hairs out of the way for him to access her more, as she guided his fingers into her, to open her up to be ready for him to make love to her, considering what she had earlier felt of his size, and of his eagerness for her.

"That too eventually, my love. Soon. Our minds seem to go in the same direction on so many things!"

He felt her move her fingers slowly and cautiously into the open side of his clothing again. She found him easily once more, grasping him around, as before, and held him gently, as he also touched and explored her even more, becoming more and more excited, knowing where this was leading.

She moved closer to him as though to try and bring those two parts closer together, and with but one intent; finding each other.

He was nervous, trembling with excitement, and it showed in his voice. He was close to coming.

"You are very beautiful, my love; far more beautiful than ever I might expect to attract or wed. I am but a poor specimen of a man, with a clouded history. The only thing I might have to recommend me is that I love you without reservation. I can easily look after you, you know? I am very wealthy, though I do not show it, or boast about it as others do. Except I suppose I am boasting now in a way.

"I do not place much store by riches, though I am glad to have them, but I do value those persons I am close to. People are more important than things.

"My servants would look after us both so very well! I, shall look after you. That, will be my sole responsibility."

"And to make me with child, Robert."

He laughed nervously at her disingenuousness.

"That, too."

He spoke on, trying to take his mind off that other, as she handled him more confidently, gradually reconciling her fears, with that need to have him make love to her, and wanting to get a start on... *'making her with child'*, as she'd said.

He continued talking, trying to take his mind off this other, that was happening to him under her touch.

"I am not sure how wealthy my father was when he died, or even what I added to it from my prize money.

"I have an inkling to buy a large property somewhere close by, in the country, out of the city, where we can romp naked on the lawns in the moonlight. There will, of course, be a large hedge, around it for privacy. Or we can lose ourselves in the maze and make love in there. As only we, shall know the way in or out, we need not fear being discovered.

"We shall raise numerous children, with you as my wife, and their mother."

He recognized that he should not have said so much. That thought of being on lawns with her, and both of them naked in the moonlight, did not help his composure.

She continued to hold him as she felt his fingers moving along her in turn, exploring gently, as she opened up his clothing even more. Kissing him as he kissed her.

"Money is not important Robert. Happiness is! I know I would be happy with you, but I was not sure that I might become so ambitious as to expect marriage!"

He paused and kissed her upon her breasts, leaving the listening-for-others-approaching, to her.

"Your happiness is my main reason for wanting to marry you. I seem to make you happy. I have never been happier myself than when I am with you, even without, this, that we are doing."

"You do make me happy, Robert! I have never been so happy in all of my life as I have been over the last few days. Nor so excited as I am now!"

He could feel that for himself. She had become even warmer, more moist, and had opened up more to him, as his fingers had moved along that softly-receptive, warm, and slippery groove, and slid so easily once more, into that other entrance, exploring that more deeply too, with her distracted with what she was feeling, and doing to him.

"Good, then that's settled then. We marry in the morning."

She did not question that.

"I am glad that is out of the way because your father and James both gave their approval when I so boldly and rashly broached it with them a few days ago, so there is no going back on it now."

She stopped again.

"You asked my father… for his permission… a few days ago?"

"Yes, my love. I did. I freely confess it. I was in a hell of a bind, having fallen insanely in love with his daughter, and I was not sure how I was going to control myself around her."

He chuckled, recalling his audacity.

"He didn't understand at first. What father would? His first inclination, I am sure, was to kill me, take my body down to the river, and see the last of me. James would have helped him, too."

This was all news to her.

He started, as her grasp had slowly tightened on him, the more he revealed.

She laughed apologetically, sensing what she had done.

"Sorry! I did not mean to hurt you!"

"You didn't hurt me, my love! You are moving 'him', more than is wise at the moment, and you are causing another problem for me! If you do any more of that I will certainly 'come', and I would rather I were in you, where I should be, when that happens."

She wanted that too.

She sensed a gentle pulsating, in that part she held, and was curious about it, but she stopped moving him. It had seemed the right thing to do with the skin being so soft, and wanting to slide up and down that hard shaft, the way it did.

He tried to put his mind back to what he was saying, and to take his mind off that other, that threatened to become front and center in his mind.

"Yes, my love, I did ask him. James was there too. They were both shocked and even outraged, that I dared have such gall, but eventually they came around and approved. Reluctantly, of course. They were so much put off balance at the sheer impudence of such a scambling, shambling rattle as myself, daring to think he might want to marry you, the most treasured possession they either of them have, and thinking I might take it for my own, with no more than a few words in a simple ceremony, and after knowing you for such a little time."

He breathed out slowly, thankful to have got past that earlier moment without an accident.

"That I could achieve something so valuable with such little effort on my part, is still unthinkable. We all know that she; the woman I set my heart upon, is easily the most beautiful woman in all of London, and they did not at all like, that I had made that same discovery within minutes of meeting her. How lucky I am that all of London does not know you too, as I know you!"

He hesitated.

"But do you not approve that I asked him? You seemed startled. You squeezed…"

"I did not expect it, Robert, and you took me off guard. Was that why the twins were curious, and laughing the way they were?" She chuckled, thinking of what they had known before she did.

"Probably. I think I may also have been undone, and I did not have your dress covering me as much as we'd thought.

"Everyone in the house, but you and your mother know of my feelings for you, and that we are about to marry, but now you do, so she is the only one who does not know. She will not find out until after the fact, and maybe not very soon even then."

"But…we marry in the morning, you said, Robert?"

"In the morning, early. Yes, my love. Everyone is sworn to secrecy."

"But how could you arrange it so soon?"

"I didn't. Your father, your brother, and James did, while we were out walking in the city and by the river." She had fallen silent again.

"As soon as we can arrange it—a day or two—you will come and live with me in my home. George is already there, and your sisters will be there too, just as often as they wish to be."

"But surely my father did not approve of anything happening so quickly! How could he? I know he seeks the best for me, but what is the best, and what is achievable, are often two very different things!"

Her hand moved further down, along him, and then returned to the very top and investigated over the tip of his erection, not letting him rest for a second.

"There is something wet, and very slippery here, Robert. Very slippery! Would that be to ease its passage into… into me… into my body?"

"Yes, my dear, that is what it is about!"

He was also rapidly learning, that no man should try to conduct a conversation at the same time as what she was doing to him, but he tried to ignore it. Unsuccessfully.

He swallowed hard, becoming agitated with her firm touch.

"Your father. He did not approve at first. I had a devil of a job to persuade him; and not for the reasons you might think. He knew that I was not prone to impetuous stupidity, or paying attention to social niceties.

"He demanded to know all about me, down to even the finest details of my flawed character, and every skeleton in my closet before he might even think about letting me get closer to you after that second night, never mind about approving of me. The inquisition was more gentle I think, than what happened to me. I took more heart at his probable response when he even wanted to know how I might be able to look after you, as he would like for you to be looked after.

"It was an uncomfortable interview, except for that last part! I sensed that I had persuaded him when we got onto that part of it. Until then, I think he was very inclined to hurl me out of the house as-soon-as possible, and forbid me ever to darken its door again! But then he thought of you and how we both needed to rescue you from this… this difficult place.”

Rebecca had also had a strange conversation with her father too, that morning after that, asking her how she felt about Mr. Hannan, and now, it was mostly explained.

“When did you have this conversation with him?” She was becoming strangely agitated, and moved herself more strongly, putting her legs much further apart to allow him greater access still, and pulling him down to kiss her on top of her breasts and then all over them.

He would not survive much more of this.

“You can go a little deeper and more firmly into me there, Robert, with your fingers, you will not hurt me – yes, that’s better, even a little more! You should move down the chair yourself, too, Robert, and that will make it easier for both of us! I think I know what must be done.”

He noticed that she had become flushed, and more than a little breathless at what they were both doing to each other. She hurriedly, and perhaps even clumsily in her haste, undid the buttons at the other side of his trousers, folded the opening away, liberating him entirely from his clothing, to stand proud and erect, as she learned much more of his now free-standing member. She needed to know more.

He was nervous, but did not object.

She spoke gently into his ear to reassure him.

“Don’t worry Robert, I will hear anyone approaching for some time before they get here, and if not, I can easily hide you with my dress, as I have done before. Except I will need to have it on to do that.”

She had not given sufficient thought how the two of them would be arranged together if she did that. It would be too bloody obvious what they would be doing.

She paused.

“However, I have a better idea about how we can be more private, Robert, without any fear of being discovered doing this.”

She took his hand and drew him with her to his feet, helping him put himself away, having no shyness about touching and holding him now, even as he touched her in turn between her legs.

"I will need my dress on, Robert, but not for long."

The culmination of all desires.

He dropped her dress over her head and brought it down on her, kissing, and holding her breasts before hiding them away.

She stood with her hands on his shoulders at first, holding her dress there, hoping and expecting he would do that, before she let it drop around her, then feeling him touch under it too, smoothing his fingers along her still sensitive vulva, unable to leave her alone after all of the previous excitement, kissing her.

She hugged him, knowing how he was feeling.

"I hope you can be patient, Robert. There are other places we can be private with each other, but we will need to take all of our things with us, as though we had gone into the garden or even for a walk, despite the weather."

"I will try to be patient, my love, but it is getting more and more difficult for me, with so much promised."

She giggled. It was becoming difficult for her too. She was becoming as eager as a little girl upon her birthday, knowing that there were many presents to open, but not sure what they were, or which one she would open first. Except she did know which present she would get, this time. She had felt it earlier.

"Robert, I will ask you to go across the room, and open that wainscoting section, as it would be, if we had gone into the garden and lcft it ajar to get back in, and then we shall leave this room."

She explained what she intended.

"There are four, attic-rooms off this corridor, beyond the stairs. There is this one, and the one we use for storage. At the far end of the corridor there are two others, both mostly empty. One of them catches the morning sun and, despite the rain, it will be bright in there, at this time of day. They are usually locked, but I have keys for all rooms in the house.

As Robert opened the wainscoting and then pulled it closed again, as she'd instructed, without latching it, she opened a drawer in the table and took out a key from the many there, before leading him out of that room, carrying their outdoor shoes and their other things with them.

Nobody should learn where they actually were.

He hoped no one would see the ruffled, and desperate state he was in; his shirt pulled up, his trousers still partially undone, unable to completely hide that part of him away, the way he was.

She knew all about him and the difficulty he had. She had even been brave enough to check for herself, feeling him poking out of the side. She walked ahead of him to hide that part of him that betrayed his feelings for her if her sisters, or James came up the stairs without being heard, though it would be obvious to anyone what the circumstance was, if they saw either of them.

No one came, and no one saw them as they moved silently along that corridor.

She let them into a far room, carefully locking the door behind them They were now, safe from scrutiny. The window overlooked only the roofs of other buildings.

Robert could see that there was a wingback chair in the window space, a round table, a dining room chair, and even a day bed.

She may have planned this, earlier. He could see scuff marks in the light dust on the floor, where those things had recently been dragged around after being brought into this room from along the corridor.

Without saying anything, she led him across to the day bed, knowing exactly where it was, turned to face him, letting her dress drop from her shoulders again, tossed it onto the day bed, and did not hesitate to start on his clothing.

With promise of what he knew she intended for him after those tormenting moments of earlier, he helped her, fingers all turned to thumbs in his eagerness, throwing his clothing onto the bed with her dress. He waited to see what else she planned to do for him, letting her decide how they would go forward with this next intimate step; not wanting to overwhelm her as his instincts shrieked at him to do.

He felt her hands check over his body, hesitating for a brief moment when she touched him, 'there', finding out how that difficult item for any woman, stood out from his body. Her fingers traced along it, assessing it in some way, then rested her hand along it, under it, lifting, possibly gaining a picture of its size in her mind.

She did not run screaming from the room. The thought amused him.

Everything about this part of him took her breath away and concerned her. It was too long, and far too big around to fit easily into her body without a lot of struggling and discomfort, if not pain for her, but there had to be a way, and something she could do, she hoped.

Rebecca was not one to be intimidated by what might seem impossible for long, and tried not to seem intimidated, but used both hands to learn more, discovering his testicles, as she held them cushioned in the palm of her hand, while she continued to discover more about the other, pulling the skin back down along it, learning everything she could.

He moved his hand from her breasts to her shoulders for that, before returning to hold her breasts again, leaning in to kiss her, not sure how much more he could take, before he melted under this ache that he felt for her and 'came'.

"Sit here, Robert."

She learned where the hard chair was and sat him upon it as she stood in front of him, feeling him pull her closer so that he could kiss her on her naval and anywhere else she would let him, as he touched her between her legs, but she had other plans.

She knew what she wanted, and slowly went onto her knees in front of him, while holding him on the top of his legs, just back from his knees, moving his legs apart as he always wanted to do with her.

"You will need to sit farther forward, Robert."

She helped pull him to the front of the chair, as she moved closer to him, pushing her hand under his testicles to hold them again.

"Tell me about each of these things, Robert, as I touch them. Remember that I have never known about, or touched anything like these before, though I once heard them breeding a mare down in the stable-yard.

"Some of what they said was about these, and this. The things they said; the descriptions, the swearing, the noise of hooves on the flagstones, and the snorting and heavy breathing from the animals and the squealing of both mare and stallion, suggested a lot of activity, excitement, and even frustration. I was glad that I was not down there (it was not a place for a woman to be), but I would have like to have seen what happened between them. It did not seem to take long, once they'd started.

"I heard one of the scullery maids after that; say she had watched it from the window, and that that monstrous part of the stallion was at least fifteen inches long. Longer than from her elbow to the tips of her fingers."

Rebecca giggled. "Thank god you are not that big, but…! That maid did not understand how the stallion got all if it into the mare with just one mad push, and that he must have hurt her, and then she spoke about her own experiences with a man in the same way.

"I should not have listened."

She stopped there.

"I learned about your face, last time we did this, Robert, and I now need to know about your body, and about these, as I think that I am going to become very familiar with them."

She would, indeed.

He leaned in and kissed her "If I survive this moment, my love, I will tell you whatever I can." And even if he didn't survive. It would not be the end of the world, just the first hurdle in a long race.

She laughed, puzzled by his suggestion that he might not survive what she was doing. Would he 'come'? That must be what he meant.

Robert coughed and cleared his throat.

"Robert!" She seemed amazed. "They moved in my hand. They lifted, jumped, when you did that."

He touched her by the side of her face.

"My coughing did that. Those items in your hand, my love, are my testicles, also known as, my balls. They are very delicate and tender and should never be handled roughly."

"They feel it. I will take very good care of them and never handle them roughly, Robert. They are very soft, and they move easily in this fleshy little sack. Two of them, about the size of walnuts."

"You must never squeeze them my love, or you will inflict horrendous pain on me, and it will take a lot of time to recover."

"Then I won't, but they move so easily in here. If they are so tender, why do they hang loose, like this, outside of your body? They should be protected within it."

"That, is a question I cannot easily answer, except that they are where my sperm is manufactured, so there needs to be the shortest path from them to the tip of my penis, before I ejaculate deep into you."

She liked to hear that, but was also concerned... *'Deep into you'.*

"I would like to experience that, Robert."

"Soon, my love. It will happen very soon." Too damned soon. Yet at the same time, not soon enough.

"The skin around them is very loose."

He took her hand and showed her how to pinch the loose skin on the surface of his testicles, and to pull that sack around to show her how loose, it really was, amazing her, that doing that was not painful for him, but it wasn't.

He moved to hold her shoulders, letting her continue to discover more about him. He was unable to resist moving his hand to touch her breasts and to lean in and kiss her, trying not to distract her.

Everything she did, excited him. No matter what it was. She would always excite him, so he should just get used to her touching him. Though he never would.

"The skin is loose, like that, because the room is still so very warm. If it were cold, then that little sack would tighten up around them, shrivel up, and pull them closer to my body." She accepted that, wanting to feel that for herself, and moved on to touch that other proud item in front of her.

"And this, Robert." She seemed overawed by it as she held it, touched it, discovered what she could about it.

"Is it always this big… and so stiff and unyielding?'…she moved it… "and hard, yet the skin on it is so easily moved, and so soft."

"No, my love, he is not always this big; only when you touch it, or you excite me. Just like my balls, when it becomes cold and there is nothing to excite me, then it becomes much smaller. The blood recedes from it, and it retreats into that foreskin; the loose skin up around the head, and along it, becoming only an inch or two long, at most."

She tried to envisage that.

"Like that sheath on the stallion?"

The maid must have been very graphic in her awed description.

"Yes, my love, almost like that." He was becoming agitated and breathless as she touched and held him.

"My phallus, or my penis, is only the way it is now, when I am close to you... think of you... or you touch and hold me like this. Or when I am in your body."

She repeated those names again.

"Phallus. Penis. But is it not also called, a 'cock'? I heard those men in the yard shouting something about... 'let him get his cock into her, you fool, don't get in the way or he'll fuck you up instead, when he mounts her." She could easily recall such conversations.

She hesitated. "But I don't think I was meant to hear that."

"No, my love, you weren't, and that last word, 'fuck', should never be used in polite company."

"Oh! What does it mean?"

"it is a very impolite way of saying, 'making love'. the actual physical aspects of that union. It is referred to as 'fucking'."

"Oh!"

She repeated those names again, and traced the skin connection between his testicles and his phallus, then slowly moved to the top of it, feeling it coming more to life under her touch, and feeling Robert's touch upon her, pause, as his breath caught.

"Did I do something to hurt you, Robert?"

He responded very gently, though he felt like being anything but gentle.

"No, my love. Your touch is exciting me to an extreme."

"Should I stop?"

He breathed steadily.

"No, please don't. But try not to move that skin on my shaft, there, quite as energetically as you are doing. That, is dangerous and will drive me along too far, too fast." She chuckled... not fully understanding.

"I may lose control if you do that, or grip me so hard."

He took a couple of deep breaths, then stood up, holding her breasts as he encouraged her to her feet.

"Come, we shall change places for a while, as we did that first night. It is now my turn to learn more of what I can about you."

"You touched me often enough earlier there, Robert, I thought you would already know all about me."

"I will never know enough about you there, or touch you enough anywhere on your body in a thousand years. I will never tire of touching you."

She understood that. She felt the same about him.

"Not, that it will help my condition. I doubt anything would help that, short of my making love to you." Not even ejaculating, which he was so close to doing.

She changed places with him as they moved around each other, touching, pausing at what they were learning, feeling him kneel on the floor in front of her, moving her legs apart, leaning in to kiss her breasts, and then her, before he sat back on his heels.

She waited, to feel what he would do; flinching, and letting out a small cry as he touched her, opening up her Labia to his inspection, not helping him at all to retreat from the excitement he felt for her.

She detected his difficulty, resting her hands on his shoulders as he gently touched along her vulva, coming back to suckle at her breasts, kissing them, taking her nipple and most of her arcola into his mouth, startling her again, not knowing which area of her, most-interested him from one moment to the next, while she was not sure what he would do to her, next.

She moved forward, putting her legs as far apart as she could, denying him nothing.

"Describe what you are touching, Robert, please, as you did with your own body when I touched you."

"I will, but a woman is so very different from a man; so much more interesting and intriguing." She wasn't prepared to believe that anything could exceed her interest in him and those parts of his. "Almost every part is different." He sighed heavily.

"You have these outer, firm 'lips'—the labia majora"—he traced them out, teasing gently at them as he ran his fingers just inside them, setting her squirming—"which I do not have, protected by hair… which I do have, of course.

"Inside of these, are these even more fleshy and soft tissues—the inner lips; the *labia minora*." He moved his fingers gently along them, sighing heavily at the emotions they caused in turn. "These are protected in this delicate space of your vulva, by the outer lips. At the top of the vulva, just below the top of it, is your urethra, out of which you pee.I also have a urethra, which I will show you soon.

"I will let you hold him while I pee when we next go into the garden, and you can direct where I pee, but I am afraid that if I let you do that, I will not be able to pee for long. My penis will not pee when I become as hard as I always will when you touch him."

She could not help but laugh, envisaging that strange circumstance. He would not be able to help her that way. All she could do was to squat. Nothing dignified about that!

He touched her again.

"Just above your urethra, is your clitoris, a small and delicate, fleshy part of you that is even as sensitive for you, as my penis is for me when you are the one to touch me."

He touched it, startling her at its sudden sensitivity. Then he leaned in and kissed it, playing with it with his tongue, driving her wild in turn.

"I did not know that, Robert, and never felt that before. But how would I know that. A woman does not need to know these things. It is not done. We are taught never to touch ourselves there."

She laughed. "If I did not listen in to the conversations in the scullery, I would know so little. I still know far too little, considering how much I am learning from you. How is it that you know all of this, Robert?"

"I know it, because every part of a woman's body, haunts a man. He cannot stop thinking about it, whenever he meets a woman; especially a woman like you." He sighed again. "Unlike a girl, or a woman, a man cannot avoid touching his body there, and learning all about it, when he pees, or…"

She waited. "Or what, Robert?"

"Boys, tend to play with themselves and learn to excite themselves to become erect, deliberately, when they masturbate and make themselves 'come'. It is pleasurable to do that, but it is only a fraction of the pleasure that making love to a beautiful woman, is."

She would not ask.

"I have wanted to learn everything about your body, Rebecca, from that first moment I met you."

She chuckled, understanding that now. Men were very strange.

He confessed his first failing with her.

"That first vision I had of you, stole my breath, and my wits, completely away. You were sitting in your window, with it open, and your feet raised to the window ledge with the late sun shining full upon you." She waited for him to continue.

I saw you reflected in the window; even magnified by the glass, but I saw, not just you… I saw everything about you under the edge of your dress too; all of the disturbing detail. I saw all of this, of you… here."

He leaned in, and kissed her to show what he was talking about.

"You drove me mad at that very moment. and then, after that, you captivated me with your artlessness, your conversation, simplicity; your beauty." He sighed at having dared admit that earlier part, and showed himself to be a truly reprehensible character.

"Please try to forgive me, Rebecca."

She touched his head. "Obviously, I must forgive you Robert. We have moved so much further than that now, yet I am pleased that you could tell me."

"I felt sure you must know what I could see of you under your dress, and what I was looking at, and so much wanted to touch, and would insist I leave. But you didn't. I'm glad you didn't."

"How relieved I am that I didn't know, Robert, or I may have misjudged you. But I was interested in everything about you too.

"We seem to have infected each other the same way. You may have noticed, when I got you to help me go down to the garden. We learned a lot about each other as we maneuvered on that small landing. You were excited for me even then. I felt it against me. I even began to understand the effect we were having on each other. It happened even more in the garden when we sat together with out legs touching.

"Do you remember that I asked you, if you would kiss me?"

"How could I forget?" He leaned in to kiss and mouth at her breasts again, as he moved them with his face between them, wanting to end his life exactly there, between them, when that time came for him, or was planted within her. Or both. Disturbing thoughts.

"I knew, long before then, but that was a turning point."

She paused, so Robert took that as his cue to continue, becoming more and more excited with what he was touching, feeling, and describing.

"And lower down… here…" he touched, putting the tip of his forefinger into her, is your vagina, where this phallus of mine will always want to go. Always. Even now."

She pulled his hand closer, letting him enter her with his second finger too, and to go even deeper into her.

"You can try with this, now, if you would like to, Robert." She reached down to touch him.

Getting ever closer.

He raised to his knees, and moved closer to her, pushing his finger aside and out of the way as he inserted the head of his penis part way into her, pushing, feeling her become tense, feeling his size and how hard it was.

However, she submerged that feeling. "It doesn't hurt yet, Robert. I will stretch, I know I will, so don't' stop."

She wanted him to continue?

"Stop me, when it becomes too much for you, my love."

"I will, Robert." She felt him moving steadily forward, into her, steadily pushing her labia aside with that very large, and insistent entity, moving only a tenth of an inch at a time, before he paused each time.

Not even that first part of him would go fully into her before he felt significant resistance, but it was close to breaking beyond that barrier of her hymen, if she still had one, with all of her climbing around in a tree, and walking half of the day, as well as enduring that Absalon moment, when Robert had first kissed her there.

If he just pushed, it would hurt her dreadfully, but then, that difficult first moment would be behind them, and they could move on together.

He sensed her difficulty. "Not yet. Not yet, my love. I do not want to hurt you, and I would. It may take a while."

Her head fell, to touch his. She was relieved, but still held him where he was, still pulling steadily at him, not wanting to let him go.

She could almost taste her disappointment.

He was far too big for her, and she was not sure how to change anything, no matter how much she wanted him into her at that moment. At least he did not pull back from her, but stayed exactly where he was, waiting for her to relax, if she could, sensing her reluctance to give up so soon. If she was not about to give up, nor was he.

She waited, concentrating, willing herself to relax, feeling him advance a little with each passing minute as they talked and kissed, or as he touched her breasts or her face. She held him him where he was, not letting him retreat.

She was of two minds; wanting him to continue pushing into her there, no matter the discomfort of something so large going into her tender body there, for the first time, no matter how long it took; and another part of her wanting him to be patient with her and to let her get used to all of this strangely wonderful relationship, with this man, coming at her out of nowhere, as he had.

She sighed, knowing it would not happen as quickly as she would like. She would still be patient.

"I have other questions to ask, Robert"

He recognized and understood her concerns, and waited for her questions.

"We need to change places again."

He was not sure how much more of this he would survive, but he did as she asked.

She sensed changes in his breathing as he sat again for her, and as she touched him.

"This 'head' that you started to touch into me with down there at my Vagina, Robert. Is this where everything happens?"

"Yes, my love. It is." His voice was also different.

"And this, where you are slippery again?" Her finger moved over his tip, sensing the urethra there and the slippery fluid, leaking from him in his excitement.

"That, is from me, and is leaking from my urethra. That is where I pee from and where my ejaculate shoots from….That slippery substance is a fore-runner of me, coming, once I go into you."

He lost power of speech at that moment, lifting her pulling her into his embrace, feeling his penis move up between her breasts as he pulled her between his legs.

Everything was going wrong! He was coming! Damn!

He groaned, breathing heavily as though he had just run a race, gasped, and froze for a second or two, before doing it all again; several times.

She felt something happening between them, not sure what it was, except… he must have come. He'd been warning her about it for a while.

She giggled nervously. "What happened Robert? Did you come?" She was not sure whether to be sad, or happy for him. He had not been in her body as he should have been.

He nodded, catching his breath.

"I came." He chuckled in relief. "It's all over you, your chest, your breasts." He kissed her. "I'm sorry about that."

He seemed relieved, so she could be too.

"I'm not."

He took her hand and showed her, letting her feel its slipperiness all over the top of her breasts and under her chin, on her neck.

She had felt it hitting her as it spurted out of him as he'd described, but was not sure.

She laughed, sitting back still holding him, feeling more of him on her fingers and her hand, feeling him still pulsing with life, but slowly retreating from that moment.

"Is that all of it, Robert?"

"Yes, my love, for a short while. He sounded content.

"What happens now? How short a while?"

"I will relax until the next time that happens, possibly in a few minutes. I depends how long it takes my body to recover. It could be as short as ten, fifteen minutes, or long as half an hour if we continue what we are doing. Otherwise, not until we pick up again where we left off."

"Soon, then. A few minutes."

She decided not to let him go, feeling some other changes. "You are not as hard as you were, Robert."

"No. He will relax too, and shrink a little after that strenuous exercise, that romp, though not a romp within your garden, yet."

"Robert?" She had so many things to ask, but he had no patience with that.

He kissed her and pushed his hands behind her, lifting her to straddle across his knees, splaying her legs apart, as he directed his phallus at her, moving it along her vulva, to wait for that next time, as they touched each other.

"You are becoming noticeably smaller now." She inched herself forward on his legs, closer to him, and tried to put him into her again, where he had been before, reaching behind her to do that under her, feeling him get a beginning again.

She would soon get used to things like this. It was easier now, more slippery with what he'd done, and he went into her a little deeper than before.

"You may be able to go into me now, Robert. You have gone farther than before." She sounded excited. "I would like you to try and go into me again, please, Robert; really try, and I think it would help if we were lying down this time with you on top of me." She'd heard that maid say that it was much easier that way, with the man on top of her, pushing into her.

She got to her feet, pulling him with her and they moved onto the top of the day bed, moving their clothes to one side out of their way.

She knew what she wanted to have happen now, and would not hesitate.

She did not need to persuade him any further, but took hold of him and pulled him between her legs, as she laid back under him, guiding him to where he had been earlier, wiping some of the fluid from her chest and smearing it into her vagina, with more of it smeared along him, feeling him pushing at her again; at her vagina, getting more of a start, now that he was even only a little smaller.

"It doesn't hurt, Robert. Keep pushing, you are sliding into me, now."

She breathed through her mouth as he pushed, following her directives, feeling her pulling at him even harder, feeling him moving steadily into her without hesitation.

He was still hard enough to make headway, and he was going into her slowly and much more easily now.

She changed her hold to his hips and behind him, pulling at him even better, as he pushed.

"Do not back away, Robert, do not come out of me now. Keep going don't stop, you are going in." She sounded both surprised and happy.

He slowly slid into her, knowing that he would also recover, and become as hard as iron again, in just a matter of seconds, now that he was where he had always wanted to be since first meeting her.

"I can go no farther my love. I am fully into you now." He was also surprised, equally excited to feel that.

"I know." She was jubilant. "I have you in me, Robert. At last. I have all of you now, where you should be." She reached up and stroked his face. "Now lie on me, upon my breasts as I hold you, kiss me. We do not need to move until morning."

She chuckled at having succeeded. "When will you come again?"

"I think I am already coming again, my love, even now."

She sensed that for herself feeling him growing again, but this time, within her, and he was beginning to move excitedly, as he continued to push into her.

Suitably awed.

She rejoiced, as they lost themselves kissing each other, their mouths locked over each other, breathing fire all over each other's faces, like a pair of dragons.

She had never been so conscious of life, or of love, until this very moment, as Robert came, again; the first of many times in her now, before they needed to part.

She seemed to be suitably awed.

"But fortunately, not too much like a horse, as I once heard a man described, in that part of him!"

She heard him swallow nervously, almost a gulp, and noticed that his breathing had become a lot more labored as she detected other changes in what she held. He strove to concentrate, to be able answer her question as to when he had broached the subject of their marriage with her father.

"The second night I was here, my love. I know I left it for far too long a time, for it began to seem like a lifetime since I had learned it for myself." They began to kiss each other in the excitement of the moment. She felt him flex a little, and move even further down the seat, as he began to become entirely rigid in her hand and more excited in his breathing. There were changes in him that excited *her* too. They separated for a moment but did not back off from their activities. "You were asleep in this very chair. I had just sent you to sleep by very clumsily reading Burns" poem about a louse on a lady's bonnet. It was just as well you were not awake. Much of what I told him was not fit for the ears of a lady such as you, and some of his responses and comments at first, were quite… notable, and I dare not repeat them! But he thought about it a little, and he gradually came around to my view of things."

They kissed again. More prolonged and intense this time, before she spoke breathlessly over what he was doing to her.

"I am not a lady Robert, and I do not want to be. Look at how I have so shamelessly tormented you tonight and excited you as I did, inviting you so… so…. to touch me in this way—an unthinkable thing for a gentlewoman to allow anyone to do—and look at what I am daring to do to you! Look at what we are doing to each other now, and where this will certainly lead! I cannot imagine a lady knowing of Absalon, or some of those other things, or welcoming some of those intimacies of conversation and these other behaviors that we have shared from time to time, for we have, haven't we? Now this?"

His head dropped to her neck and she felt him nudge into the top of his dress with his head and kiss her on top of her breasts, as she gently moved it from her shoulders, and pulled the front forward a little and entirely off her, to provide him room and easy access to do so.

Her hand tightened on him even more, as she felt him becoming more excited. If she were not careful, he would soon lose his power of speech. "A well read and interesting lady in my world, *would* know of Absalon, and could even joke about it too as you did, and would not be shy with me. As you are not. But you did not ask about my third reason yet."

"You already gave me three reasons! But if there were three then I now know of a fourth, that I am finding interesting!"

He knew what she meant. "Three! No, I told you two of them. The second one had two parts to it remember – I love you and I want to marry you – that was just one."

She snuggled closer into him and encouraged him to discover more of her breasts. She allowed her hand to continue investigating his changing condition, as his did to her, and with most disturbing effects beginning to be noticed, for she was now very wet where he touched. "Then what was the third?" He had calmed a little in her hand, but not much!

"It takes two people to be in love before marriage might be considered my love. The third, was that I knew very quickly that just as I loved you, so did you love me, or I would never have dared to trespass as I so far have! I was jubilant! I need you to tell me that I was not wrong."

She spoke quietly. "You were not wrong Robert! Was I that obvious? As I am now!"

"Yes, my love. You were, and thank God for that, or I would not have survived! What a pair we were; are! James and your father just had to look at the pair of us in that chair that second night, and they decided they could not just murder me and dispose of my body in the river as they had rapidly planned, because it was obvious that you had fallen in love with me by then too. I was dispensable, but they did not have the heart to hurt you!

"They also decided right there and then that we had better get married, and quickly, though I was the one who raised that object! I am surprised they have dared leave us alone like this for as long as they do. Surely, they know what dangerously intimate things we are likely to get up to! While we had breakfast that morning. The Absalon morning...!"

"They knew!" She leaned over and kissed him gently on the top of that part she was holding, at that memory. It was salty.   "This is **my** Absalon moment Robert!"

She repeated that kiss.

He caressed her head, and then his hands moved onto her breasts and then into that other space again. "…that Absalon morning, as we had breakfast, he showed me the special license that he had procured for us."

"So, you were *all* plotting this. When were you going to tell me?"

"I did!"

"I don't remember!"

"You should. Just after I had finished reading, Burns, I asked you to marry me, and I heard you say yes. I know I did! I think I did! So then I knew that I needed to break it to your father."

"I am not so very wise about any of this, but I suspect that something is about to happen, Robert.

You are becoming unsettled. He felt her move then beside him. She continued to hold him, but raised the front of her dress onto his chest, and moved her leg over him to straddle him with her knees on the chair on either side of him.

"I hope I am doing this right. You will tell me and guide me if I am not, won't you Robert?"

"Yes my love. You seem to know instinctively what must happen."

He knew then what she intended, and he could do nothing about it . He was very ready and too well primed himself to back away. He moved his fingers out of her, and his hand out of the way under her dress, and onto her soft and smooth buttocks as he did the same with his other hand. He felt her come slowly down upon him and he felt her moving his erect, and stiffly pulsating member slowly along that moist groove and felt it begin to enter her, as she directed him into that place. She continued to kiss him as she moved further over him, and drove him steadily into her without any obvious consideration as to how uncomfortable it might be for herself, yet perhaps it wasn't, as she continued to move down him and to engulf him totally in one smooth action. He had never felt so excited.

His gasp, and more labored breathing and his movements, matching her own, told her that this was the way that this should be done.

His hands moved slowly from behind her, up her legs and back, and then pushed gently up under the front of her dress to caress her breasts as they began to kiss more passionately. He was lost at that moment as he felt the pulsing begin in earnest this time, and would be unstoppable.

"I am going to 'come', my love!" He held off for as long as he could, then his mind exploded, along with everything else as he stiffened upon her and gasped several times as he tensed and tensed again! She rested on him as his excitement began to die and she laughed gently as they kissed.

She spoke after a few minutes of analyzing what she had just experienced for the first time, but not the last.

"That was wonderful. Now, Robert. I truly can say, that I am no longer a virgin!"

"I can guarantee that my love!" He sounded exhausted and jubilant at the same time. "I am now completely hidden, out of sight, and within you, which is the only thing that should happen to him at such a moment.

"Yes. Hidden totally in me, even as big as it is! How nice! Furthermore, I am proud to be able to say that I relinquished my once precious virginity, that I despaired ever of losing, to you, my one true love." She let her head drop to his shoulder as she savored his presence deep within her.

"It was not so very painful after all, though you are surprisingly large and very thick, for I could not get my fingers all the way around you, and it was very snug at first and quite worrisome. That was a surprising ending to it Robert. You will tell me what happened won't you? I heard you make some interesting noises too, and you moved very strongly within me. I am not sure what else I felt after that, almost a spurt from you within me, before you seemed to die under me?" He was still caressing her breasts and she liked that feeling.

"That was me, *coming* within you, my dear. I came, I ejaculated. I sent my sperm into you. You will very soon learn what happened my love. It will happen again very soon, and often, when I recover."

"Good!"

"You will find, however, that first I will eventually; some minutes from now… or maybe not, shrink and then slip from you as I relax, and then there will be a warm flood of moisture from you, that I left within you, as you sensed. I also think that as I am beneath you, that I will be likely to receive most of it on me and upon my clothing."

"The inner lining of my dress will soak it up. Don't worry."

They were both exhausted, and lay there together, as they slowly recovered. Eventually, he did begin to slip from her, which she felt as he slowly diminished within her. She stood up from him, feeling him dribble from her, and then dried him off with the inside of her dress, where it had run from her onto him, and had seen to herself, with a little help from him. She discovered that his once rampant organ was now relatively limp and relaxed, and she thought, utterly charming. There was no shyness now, for she held her dress up for him, and stood with her legs apart, as he brought the candle closer by them on the table, so that he might inspect her to be sure that they had found all that they needed to find; to clean her off with his handkerchief, and to be sure that none of it had gone onto the chair or the floor.

He took the luxury of time, to inspect more of her than he needed to, and took longer over it. She understood his interest. He touched, and even gently kissed her again there too. She did not mind, but welcomed his attention as she laughingly dropped her dress over his head to trap him there. He was now free to do with her whatever he wanted to do, and whenever. They adjusted their clothing once more to hide the other evidence of what they had done. They sat together after that, not side by side as they had earlier, but with her on his lap as they held each other close, and kissed gently as he touched her breast outside of her dress at first. He had no restraint about touching either her breasts or anywhere beneath her dress after that, for everywhere was now easily accessible to him, even her breasts, and he was welcome to do so. His attention was welcome in every way, as he sensed, by the way she gently and unhesitatingly opened herself up for him when his hand went under her dress, and he could feel that she was not only very wet, and warm, but also swollen too. He could now linger as long as he liked and investigate at will, for she always warned him when anyone was approaching.

She seemed sensitive at that moment to his touch for she moaned slightly as he touched, and became most agitated as he explored. He also found from time to time, that she in turn, would not hesitate to find out about his condition either, when the mood gripped her, and gently squirmed on him, to let him know that she knew exactly where he was and what his condition might be. Before he might know it, she would liberate him again and would sit on him as she was now, but with her dress out of the way again, and nothing between them, so that once he was firm enough he could then discover where she was, and enter her once more. It seemed that he spent more time *within* her after that, than *not* inside her. It would still be obvious what they would be doing however, if anyone came in upon them, especially if they were both flushed or out of breath.

Sometime later, James brought in a tray of tea and looked at them both as they relaxed with each other. She was asleep again, but Robert was wide awake with his thoughts, and was looking a little the worse for wear with his crumpled handkerchief beside him in the chair and her dress a little more rotated around her, than it had been. He poured the tea and placed both cups within reach on the table beside them.

"I warned you she had a mind of her own Robert, and that you would have little choice in anything! Now you know why Mr. Deming and I needed to speak at some length with you the other night. She had already told us how she felt about you, even on that first night—she cannot hide any secret from me—and what she intended. We were, needless to say, shocked, but we had not the power to deny her!" He left them alone after that telling comment.

Robert had dared say nothing! Sitting by the cups on the table was the small piece of ribbon that he had tied about the branch each time he had come into the house.

What they had just done together, was often repeated after that.

A quiet interlude in the Garden.   New Discoveries

Robert awoke, sometime later.

It was pitch black everywhere, but he had his arms around Rebecca, and they were facing each other, breathing into each other's faces.

"You are awake, Robert."

"Yes."

"We made love again." She snuggled closer into his neck as though thanking him, and at the same time being amazed by it and what had happened yet again.

"We did indeed. That was the third time." He wanted to make love to her again already, even now, but should not be greedy.

"And to think I was so worried about that, the first time."

He stroked her cheek and then let his hand discover her breast as he kissed her. "I hope I did not hurt you. Making love can be a hectic affair and quite violent."

She'd already learned that.

"Not so very much, but how can something that large… this, large"… she discovered him between them… "not go into me without there being some discomfort at first?"

It was all very strange to her, never having experienced either that, in quite that more forceful way, as she just had, or proper love before, in her life up to that point, and not sure how she had been so unaware of anything so wondrous before now.

Their previous interactions had been wondrous enough, but he had never gone into quite as deeply, or seemingly quite that hard and eager for her, as on the previous night. But she could be mistaken about that too. Her mind was in a complete turmoil, not sure what she was feeling, other than the most comforting feeling of having arrived… in life… where she most needed to be.

"No matter, Robert. Too late to worry about it now, thank goodness." She moved closer to him. "That last time was easier, and it seems to be always getting easier, as long as you go slowly. I seem better able to relax now to let you into me much easier than before, and much more easily than the first few times we did it in that chair.”

“I will always go slowly, my love.” She knew he would.

She kissed him in return. They were always kissing. It was pleasurable to be kissed.

“It is just two o’clock. I heard the clock strike downstairs just moments ago.”

They changed positions with each other, finding out what had changed. He was still aroused, but not as noticeably. He had just left her body; slipped out of her, and that was what had woken him up, but he was still hard, still wanting to go back into her.

He made a start on that, preferring to be close to her and intimate.

She adjusted her own position to accommodate him once more.

“While we were occupied, earlier, I heard James take some refreshments into that other room for when we returned. Probably, sandwiches and cakes. And wine. It has also stopped raining. We could go and eat, and then go into the garden. The rest of the house is asleep. No one will know.”

She stroked his head, feeling him pull her closer to him, knowing that he would soon be able to make love to her again, even ejaculate again; a strange and satisfying completeness, but then they might never want to leave; or eat.

Never, had she felt so happy or so fulfilled. Nothing that had happened to her since Robert had first arrived in her life, would she ever have believed to have been possible for herself.

“We can eat first, Robert, if you do not mind; sit together just as we are; touch, kiss, hold each other, as now, and then decide what we will do.

“We should put some things on when we go out; if we go out... just in case they are not all asleep, though I am sure it is very dark, so we probably don’t need to, and I can hear nothing from downstairs.”

“It is very dark.” He confirmed that for her. “No stars, no moon. Pitch black.”

He reluctantly withdrew from her, doing so, slowly. They disentangled themselves from each other, never losing contact as she held his hand; their bodies still touching almost everywhere.

She seemed to stumble. He caught her and held her around her waist.

"Oh!"

He felt her pause, and reach out for something where they had just been lying. He knew what was happening. It would happen often now.

"Robert! I feel you running from me. It must be you, considering what we did."

"It is indeed me, my love. A small part of my offering to my goddess, within her temple."

She laughed at the way he addressed her. "It feels so strange. But I don't want to lose any of you."

"There will soon be more of it; a lot more of it, so don't worry."

He found her hand holding something; reached around her from the back, and pushed his hand between her legs to catch it in his hand, feeling the damp trail down her leg as she relaxed into his touch, trying to hold him in her body, but not succeeding; realizing that she didn't need to worry. There would always be more of that, and on a regular basis.

She had his smalls, which he helped move up into her there, tucking them up between her legs to catch the rest of it, as they laughed together.

So many strange and wonderful things were happening to her that she'd never known before. Everything was new, and strange, but was also welcome, even if it did betray the expectations of their very judgmental society. However, what their society did not know, it could not judge.

He kissed her on her neck and then raised his free hand to her breast, pulling her back into him, as she leaned back in turn.

When the nagging, discomforting trickle had subsided, she led him to the door, slowly turned the key as quietly as she could and let them out into the corridor. She listened for a few moments before leading him to the attic room where they'd first met. He touched her the entire time, either her breasts, or between her legs from behind, setting her dancing excitedly ahead of him.

A candle was burning on the table, which was set with various things on it. One large dish with a glass dome, covered various sandwiches.

Robert led her to that wingback chair closest to the table, and explained that he would wait on her, placing everything they needed within reach, or helping her find it as they ate hungrily, sitting together with their legs over each other, touching, drinking from the same wineglass, neither of them saying anything for a while; kissing often, even as they were eating. Kissing everywhere they could reach.

"It is still not raining again, so we should walk in the garden and listen, and you can tell me what you see and hear, Robert. James will not come up again until daylight."

She followed him through into that cavity behind the wainscoting, feeling him reach out for her, to bring her in with him; going into her again, briefly, as they stood there, arms around each other and kissed, sensing everything about each other's bodies, and the infectious mood of it all.

He wanted her again. But the garden, first. They could even make love in the garden. They could make love anywhere now, and everywhere.

She stayed in contact with him all of the time they descended, with him vibrantly aware of her breasts touching him most of the time, and feeling the hair between her legs on his lower back as she moved down to him with each step as he waited for her. He reached back often to touch both of her soft cheeks and to pull her closer to him, before he went down another step, counting them. He knew his way about in the dark here, almost as well as she did.

There was no difference between the darkness they'd left, and the darkness of the garden, but they could immediately feel the damp and the humidity, and hear water, drip, occasionally, from the leaves, though the air was still.

It was refreshing and clean, compared with the dust of that place they had just left.

They said nothing for a while. He put his arm around her; reaching across to hold her breast; and she led him slowly around the garden.

He whispered into her ear. "There is nothing to be seen out here. Nothing."

They strolled through the wet grass as she led him farther out, reaching out to touch something familiar that she knew to be there, or feeling a low branch, heavy with water, brush her shoulder.

She stood still and listened.

Something had caught her attention. Then she half-turned and listened again.

"A smell. A strange smell. Unpleasant. And now that noise, Robert. What can it be?"

He listened too.

It sounded like… like the distant roar of a fire, or of a tidal bore making its way up an estuary. It was also getting closer to them.

"It is a downpour, my love, coming at us through the trees."

She held him still.

"We have nothing to get wet, Robert, so we do not need to retreat in any haste."

She could hear the first heavier drops spattering through the vegetation around them and then hitting them as Robert took her into his arms and they stood there.

It was not particularly cold, though the drops hit the skin hard and soon soaked their hair and their bodies.

They could hear it begin to cascade off the roof, to splatter on the ground quite close.

She took his hand and led him to stand under it, raising her face to it, though it felt painful on her breasts until they moved out of the full force of it as the heavens opened even more.

They stood there for a few minutes, reveling in the magnificence of nature; how the sound of the rain drowned out all other sounds, muted all smells, other than for that, not-unpleasant-smell of damp vegetation all around them, and then they retreated to the house.

Robert found that small towel left there for cleaning off their feet, and used it to take off most of the water from her shoulders and from her body and hair, then passed it to her to do the same for him.

He flinched when she used it to dry off that aroused part of his, discovering his state of readiness for her again. He chuckled. She would never be able to leave that alone, any more than he could not touch her breasts or anywhere else.

They climbed the stairs slowly. She waited for him, reaching back for him, taking hold of his aroused phallus—taking possession of it; hers now—feeling the change in it as he climbed to join her, then she advanced another step as he touched her in turn ahead of him between her legs.

She did not squeal or move faster when he did that now, but let him find her and touch her so gently, even pausing for him each time to discover more.

They both knew where this was going, and soon.

Would it be on these stairs, or the landing? He could take her here, where they were now, if he wanted to. Or could they wait until they got into the attic, and then would it be in that chair or against the wall, as they almost had, in that storage room not that long ago now?

They locked their arms around each other as they maneuvered on the landing, taking their time about doing anything as they kissed again. He opened the door at the top as she listened, with him nestled between her legs at the top of them, in that space where they joined her body; a space designed by nature to accomodate him there if he was not in her body.

There was nothing to hear but the rain on the roof.

They did not move for a while, just standing there, holding, touching each other, kissing, analyzing their feelings, becoming focused and eager.

Robert, lifted behind her, raising her to his waist, her legs wrapping around him, as she held him around his neck, and he climbed slowly into that dark space with her, letting her down onto the floor with him between her legs, and her under him.

It would be now!

She reached down to hold him, guiding him slowly into her vagina, moving a few hairs out of his way and opening herself as she needed to, as they kissed. She ignored the hard floor on her back, focusing only on getting him into her again, before he came, sensing that it was not far off now, after all of that playing in the garden; and as they'd dried each other; then on the stairs; and finally, on the landing.

They lay exhausted, giggling together after that as they both recovered.

She'd left his undershorts in that chair when they had fallen from her after they had done their job of soaking him up, so they were well-out-of-reach.

There would be more of him left on the floor in front of that cubby-hole, but it would dry before morning if she were to spread it around with her feet, or not let it run from her. They still had some wine to finish off and a couple of sandwiches, and they still needed to get dry, properly, and the towels were over there too, but she liked where they were now and what they were doing; again.

"How did we manage to survive without each other, before we met, Robert? How did I never know until now, what it was like to make love to you? My life was empty until you came into it."

He kissed her and gently pushed, to make sure he did not come out of her body until he was ready to.

"Let us not think of that, please. We have something else to worry about now, and that is… not leaving a trail out of here when I come out of you."

He smiled, his mind still able to function; just.

"But I don't have to come out of you." He lifted under her thighs.

"If you come up onto me again as you were when we climbed into this room, I can get us over to that chair, and anywhere else we need to be."

He felt her move her legs, as they adjusted where they were, relative to each other, bringing her legs around his waist again. holding him around his neck as he clambered to his feet with her. He walked, with her impaled upon him; his hands under her buttocks as they shuffled slowly to that chair, in the dim light from that stub of a candle.

He slowly settled back into it, without changing anything about them, other than to drop his undershorts between their bodies for that time when they did separate.

Calamity, evaded!

They had some sandwiches to eat and some wine to finish off before they needed to think of doing anything else.

Another Step Forward.

"You shall come with me Robert. We do not need to get dressed. No one will see us anywhere in the house at this time. I will show you my room and you shall stay there with me tonight. It is still raining hard and I would not like you to get soaked, trying to get home in this."

She took his hand and led him away from that attic room, leaving everything for James to see to in the morning.

They retrieved their clothing from that other room, though they did not need to bother getting dressed, and she led him quietly down onto the lower corridor, and through the house to her room, where she reached up to the top of the door and tripped the latch, known only to her, her sisters, her father, and James, to let them both in.

She felt him snuggling behind her, moving close into her, kissing her on her neck; reaching around her to hold her breasts, feeling her pause for him to do that after he'd dropped their clothing to the floor in her room; without a sound, fortunately.

He could see that there was a fire lit, though it was now dying down, leaving a bed of hot, and glowing ashes.

She closed the door behind them and turned the small wooden peg over the latch so that no-one could come in after them and surprise them.

She moved into his arms.

They had no need to hold back from each other now.

"I do hope you will not be shy, Robert, or hold back from me now. We have gone long past that."

He laughed at her preposterous suggestion. "I am not shy with you, my love. I have not been shy for many days now."

She rested her head on his shoulder, feeling him holding behind her, pulling her to him, leaning in to kiss her.

"Good. There should be a towel close by the fire for us to dry our hair better."

They did not need to be concerned about awakening anyone below her room. There was only the scullery beneath them.

She led him across to the fire, and heard him make it up from the coal scuttle there, as she sat upon the leather top of the fender, getting her back warm, always staying in contact with him.

He turned to her, seeing the fire come back to life and untied her hair to dry it as he stood in front of her, feeling her holding him in turn, encouraging him back to life, as she supported his testicles, and kissed him everywhere she could.

He tried not to stand too close to her, as he moved about to cover her entire head. He could not help but notice that her breasts moved interestingly in the firelight as he vigorously dried her hair. Everything about her, still made him breathless.

After he had dried them both, she pulled him down to the floor with her in front of the fire.

"I shall have to send a note to your brother, George, in the morning, to bring me some suitable clothing from my home."

She held his head and kissed him as he moved above her.

"The twins will come in here to dress me, so…. How will we handle that, or James? They will see you here and will know that you were here all night, but I no longer care."

"I, shall be the one to dress you, going forward from here, my love, and you shall dress me."

She gurgled, knowing what would be obvious to the entire house, if it was not already known.

"Robert, you have given me so much pleasure in the last few days, and now I must repay that in the only way I know how. Give me your hands!"

He did so, not sure what she intended. She struggled to her feet, raising him to stand with her, and stood immediately in front of him. "You do, of course, recall that first night when I explored your face and you also did the same for me, and earlier this evening?"

"Yes. How could I ever forget that?" He began to wonder what she might suggest.

"I sensed your excitement. I was excited too. We shall continue that process, now, just as we are. We can touch each other everywhere now, where we could not before, though I know we both wanted to.

"You said that you would like to kiss every inch of my body. That opportunity is now before you."

She felt him reach out to her and place his hands upon her head as they had that first evening together. He leaned in and kissed her, as her hands raised to his waist, and even behind him, holding him close, with gentle familiarity, pulling him closer to her, knowing what she could feel. They would soon need to make love again.

She sensed his excitement and was almost as breathless as he was. It excited them both that they were now able to become as intimately familiar with each other as they had long wanted to.

He moved his hands down to her shoulders and then onto the sides of her breasts. It was but a small movement to the front and onto the nipples to explore her breasts as he would always want to. She gasped in excitement at his caress and touch. Her nipples were hard under the palms of his hands. He had not noticed that so well before.

He felt the full extent of her breasts, holding them in his hands as he explored around and on top, and under them, and then moved his hands down, across, and behind her, and then back to her belly, encountering the hair he had first glimpsed, reflected in the mirror of the window those first few minutes of their meeting, with the sun shining full in upon her, warming her, and with her lower body reflected in the window.

She had known nothing of that, at the time, fortunately. They had been total strangers then, and she would have been devastated had she known what she had been revealing of herself, even by reflection, at that first moment of meeting.

He felt her move her legs apart, and then even farther, as he moved down below the hair and felt the warmth and softer moist flesh of her inner labia, that he had kissed as she had been trapped in that tree, unable to move, and that he had later touched gently as she'd sat with him.

He was nervous, and becoming breathless with anticipation feeling how well lubricated, warm, and smooth she was; for him. She wanted him to go into her again. He wanted to go into her.

At the same time, she found him, which would have been hard for her to miss. He was fully aroused by then, of course. They inevitably, moved closer together then, and kissed long, and with an excitement that neither of them had felt before in quite that way. He felt her kneel to the floor, and she pulled him down with her to lie in front of the fire together.

"Robert! I need you to make love to me again, now please, and then, afterward we shall get into bed and continue this between us, and as often as we might be allowed the privacy to do so after that, no matter where we are."

He felt her take him then, as he moved above her to kneel between her legs. She guided him into her without hesitation or concern of any discomfort.

He was very slippery by then from his own excitement, but knew better than to rush forward and hurt her, continuing to kiss and caress her with his lips upon her breasts, her neck, her face, and her lips. The excitement built in them both, as he gradually, and slowly, moved into her, feeling her embracing moistness around him in response to what they were doing.

He was not long in coming.

They lay breathlessly together after that, kissing, and then talked as they continued to caress.

She felt him gradually shrink within her over the next few minutes before he slipped from her with a gasp. They both chuckled over that, as she found him again and held him tenderly in her hand.

"Now, a lamb, instead of the raging lion you were a few minutes ago, Robert. Considering the fascination that this part of you holds for me, I am not surprised that you wanted to kiss me as you did – like Absalon – on my corresponding parts, when you had me trapped in that tree! If you would like to sleep here, in front of the fire as we are, we can do so. It is soft on the rug, and warm. Or we can sleep in my bed. It is small, but we do not need anything larger.

When she awoke at first light the next morning, she felt warmth beside her, with Robert breathing over her breasts, where she had held him for most of the night.

None of it had been a dream.

She then remembered waking with him from time to time and them making love again, and yet again.

Their preferred state together, she soon recognized, was with him lying upon her and inside of her. She explored, and discovered that he was aroused again, and even then, was beginning to awake and to move above her again to continue their lovemaking. He had been erect for most of the night, even in his sleep, as she had discovered each time she touched and held him; played with him; needing to know everything she could about this part of his that went into her body so often and so excitedly, and had such a wonderful effect on her.

She had been amazed at the wondrous climax of their activity each time, when he had suddenly become even more forceful in his penetration of her and had gasped and driven deeper into her; then feeling him ejaculate within her, so many times. It was a part of him that only she, would know now.

She heard a gentle tapping at her door, and dragged her mind back to where she was.

"Lie still Robert. I shall see to this. It is the twins." She'd recognized the way they knocked.

She moved out from under him, walking over to the door, pausing, cupping her hand beneath herself, feeling him running out of her. She stretched and moved the peg from above the door, returning to bed with Robert, and covering him entirely with the sheet to hide him, as the twins entered, looking around.

They knew what was happening, and that Robert was there under the sheet with her. They saw other signs of his presence too, and saw the trail their sister had left as they'd left the attic, and even outside of this door as they had stood there until she'd opened it, with her still dribbling onto the floor. More of it was inside, too, left there just now.

They scuffed those marks out of sight with their feet, marveling at what it meant to have a man come into their lives as Robert had come into Rebecca's. They still needed to ask her about that, what they were doing together every chance they got to be alone, and what it meant. They knew; had seen; and had overheard some of it.

"The coast is clear. You both must come and get breakfast and then we will see to getting you prepared for later."

They knew he was there with her, seeing his hands move under the sheet onto her breasts which were not entirely hidden! They could see his hands full upon her breasts. The devil! How could they not know that they were being observed?

His clothing was just inside the door, with his boots, and her dress was where she had dropped it. That sheet should be changed from the bed, too.

"Mama will not be up before noon. Not after what James put by her table for her to drink last night, so you need not tiptoe about. We'll see you downstairs when you manage to get dressed." They left, giggling at everything they had seen.

A simple ceremony.

George brought Robert a change of clothes from his home, after an early message was sent to him. He also came over in Robert's carriage. It would carry them back to Robert's home after the ceremony, where he and Rebecca would settle into a far better environment than this house had ever been for her, and where everything was already prepared to greet her.

Robert would escort her around his home and introduce her to his servants. She would have total freedom to come and go as she pleased. He would also escort her around his garden. His mother had been as fond of roses, as Rebecca herself was, so she would find a home, away from home, surrounded by all of those things that she loved, including free and unlimited access to the pianoforte and even a harpsichord, played also by his mother when she had been alive. The house would come to life once more and soon, there would be…. But that was looking farther into the future. Though they may already have got a start on the first of their family. They both hoped so.

James took Robert's change of clothing upstairs and let Rebecca know that it would be just outside of her door. His sole interest was for the happiness and welfare of Rebecca. He would not ask where they had both spent the night. Some things were better not pried into, for propriety's sake. He knew, what he knew, and would not judge what he could see was not wrong. There would be no harm come to Miss Rebecca from what was happening between them, even though it had run away with them both, but only good, could come of a love like the one they both shared, and he would not adversely judge anything that had been so totally necessary.

Everyone knew enough to leave the happy pair alone, to bathe, and to dress each other in peace.

However, once Robert had got himself dressed after seeing to Rebecca, the twins intruded once more, sensing their moment, and shooed him out of the room as they saw to final preparations with their sister. A man would never be able to see to her as they could, seeing to her hair and making other final touches to the wedding dress that had once been their mother's on her wedding day, as they got her dressed in it.

As they saw to her, they had no difficulty asking Rebecca all of those questions that sisters, so close to each other, were always able to ask, feigning shock at what she happily told them about the intense interest that a man seemed to have with a woman's body… especially when it was unclothed, and without any hint of shame that it had run away with them as fast as it had (there was nothing to be ashamed of. Everything had been necessary and called for), though they had already seen more than enough for themselves from time to time as they had blundered in upon the two of them, intimately engaged as they sometimes had been, and as they had investigated more of the attic rooms and discovered the extent and the intensity of their relationship.

Their sister was happy. She was more than happy. There was nothing else to say.

They had never seen Rebecca so happy, but she had never been unhappy either, no matter what fate had thrown at her. They also had a thousand questions to ask.

They were the ones who were frequently in society and who got out and about, yet it was their housebound sister who had been ensnared into love, though it was difficult to envisage exactly who had done the ensnaring, and right under their mother's nose too, and with their father's eager approval. It was not worth agonizing about. It had happened. Water under the bridge.

They were well-adjusted young women and did not see their sister as their mother saw her, but sought only to help her however they could. Jealousy or resentment were not part of their characters. What had happened to their sister, would soon happen to them, as it did with most women, and always in different ways, though with the same eventual outcome, so what did it matter if that happened sooner, rather than later?

Their father had been desperately searching for a way to protect his eldest daughter from the vicissitudes and cruelties of a society that viewed blindness as such a horrendous affliction (and possibly infectious), as well as protecting her from her mother, suspecting what she was capable of doing, to hurt Rebecca, in her utter shame and mindless desperation.

Robert had been a god-sent opportunity coming at just the right moment in time.

Any concerns about his sincerity, or the feelings that existed between Rebecca and him from the very beginning were soon put aside.

'For the greater good'. Even though that highly subjective consideration had also led to much pain and misery when the inquisition had reigned, and witches had been burned at the stake; virgins had been sacrificed on altars; hearts torn out to propitiate the gods that ruled their lives, and all, to ensure the continuity of the life cycle; abundant crops, fertility, absence of disease, and to hold the terrible forces of evil at bay. Too often, the forces for good, in their diligence, did far more damage than ever a thousand devils could have done, but that was easily ignored. After all, the sun still rose each morning and shone down upon them; the rains still came, the crops still grew, and all was good with the world.

Robert did not see Rebecca in the way that her mother did. He had not seen any affliction, or infirmity, but had seen her through the eyes of love, seeing a charming and accomplished young woman who may have lost one of her five senses, but who more than made up for that loss, in her intelligence, her feeling and love of everything around her, and in her beauty, as well as in the acuity of her remaining senses, as well as in her common-sense-approach to life.

Rebecca was his equal in every way, and his superior in others. It was only natural that they would be drawn to each other.

The strictures of their usual society, which would have been incensed to have learned how quickly things had moved forward between them in an intimate way, could not be applied to them. They were both outside of that society, and both, were hurting from what had happened to them before they'd met each other; him in warfare, and her, in the family setting, feeling and knowing that her mother had turned against her and wanted to hide her from society, and to behave as though she no longer existed.

They were both above those kinds of consideration of morals, or of what was proper. *'What was proper for them'*, was all that mattered.

Just as well. It had been too late for either of them after that first meeting, when Robert had first laid eyes on her and had spoken with her.

When Rebecca's sisters brought her down to the breakfast parlour, a hush fell over everything.

The twins saw the look of utter shock upon their father's face, but Rebecca sensed it. All three of them moved toward him.

"Father?" Rebecca moved into his arms. "What is wrong?"

He held her close, shedding tears into her hair, unable to speak for almost a full minute.

"It is you, my love. Though nothing is wrong. It is right, for the first time in far too long. You are so beautiful. When you came through that door as you did, you took me back twenty years and more to when I married your mother." He stroked her hair.

"She was wearing that same dress. She looked then, as you now look, and was just as happy."

He was still choked up over that.

"When you walked in, just now, I thought I was seeing her again, just as she was then. I have never seen two women look so much alike. We were so in love. Except now, I am in love with two such women. With four, if the truth were known." He took in all three of his daughters.

Yes, he still loved his wife, despite what she had put them all through.

However, he hadn't seen that woman for many years now.

"No matter. We cannot and should not dwell in the past. This is now your day, my love. The one consolation that I have, apart from your undoubted happiness, is that you are now safe with the man you love, and will be able to leave this difficult environment. It may just improve for you both." For Rebecca and for his wife, though they would not tell her anything of this.

"We have some hours before your mother is likely to be stirring, but it never pays to assume anything where your mother is concerned, so we should move forward with this marriage, get it all completed, legally seen to, and then we shall all have breakfast before you need to leave us.

"Already, I feel as though a major weight has been lifted from my shoulders. The twins have packed most of your clothes into trunks and they will go with you for a few hours.

"The house will be so empty and dull without you and George, and even more so when the twins visit you as they are already clamoring to do, though we must learn to give you time to yourselves.

"The reverend is in the front parlor with his license, and the parish register. He shall have breakfast with us after, and a glass of port to fortify him for the rest of his day."

He turned to Robert.

"You are a lucky man, Robert. I decided I would kill the man who ever tried to take my Rebecca from us; but having met you and seen the effect you had on her, and she upon you, I find that all I can do now, is to give you my blessing and to thank you for rescuing her from this. For rescuing us all, in a way."

He led the small party into the front parlor where the vicar was already waiting for them.

Both parties had reached the age of majority, so there was no difficulty with parental approvals or anything like that, and the group was a small one with relatives of the bride, but only a single friend on the groom's side. Though everyone seemed to be his friend in this case.

"We should get this out of the way and then celebrate, after. My wife's habits are not always predictable, or certain. Though it does not matter so much now. We have drawn her teeth. However, the less she knows of this, the better."

They celebrated silently, but with a sense of having triumphed.

Rebecca would leave this house and stay with Robert now. His carriage was waiting for them outside.

She would not be likely to be missed by her mother for even a day or two, or even several days, and no one would say anything of this to tell her.

She may notice that the house was quieter overall, with the twins also being away more often and for an extended period, visiting their sister, and they were made as welcome there, and were as comfortable, as they were in their own home; and the tension would be gone.

Most of them had but the one thought.

Rebecca was now safe.

Noticing a Difference.

Mrs. Deming noticed nothing for almost two days, before she said anything to her husband over their lunch. The house seemed too quiet and it seemed to nag at her, like an itch that one could not scratch, and she needed to know why that was; clearly agitated by something.

"Where are the twins?"

She bit at her biscuit, and then sipped at her coffee, trying to understand the silence of what seemed to be an empty house.

He smiled at her, contented at last that Rebecca was safe, but in a way he had not been able to anticipate coming at them as suddenly as it had.

Of course she would have noticed a difference by now, and would ask.

At least Rebecca was happy and had moved it all forward for herself and Robert, as she'd needed to, without concern for morality or restraint, and never mind any words of caution from anyone. She had no intention of losing that one opportunity presented to her by accident.

And thank god, she had.

"They are visiting a friend, my dear."

He did not need to say more or give any more details, but she persisted, as he knew she would.

"Who?"

"One that you do not know well, if at all. A recent… a very recently married acquaintance—her husband dotes on her; a girl of good character, gentle, soft spoken; remarkably accomplished in every way."

He could vouch for that. It was their own sister they were visiting.

"What name? I should know who all of their friends are. I hope she is respectable. They should have asked me first, for me to approve."

"You were not awake my dear. They asked me instead." He passed her another biscuit.

"I know the husband well, and his family. The wife also, is from a well-known family."

He knew that too, as it was his own family.

"What name?"

"The Hannan's, my love. Rutledge Gardens. A respectable part of the city." She had heard that name. The family was well known, though the son had been a bit of a rebel, from what she'd heard.

"And her name?"

"Mrs. Hannan. Mrs. Robert Hannan.

"Her, name, Reginald. Her own name?"

He struggled… "You know, I know that name almost as well as I know my own, but for the life of me at this moment, it escapes me."

She threw down her napkin in exasperation at her husband.

He continued.

"The twins will be home just after supper... I think... unless they are invited to stay another night, and then you can ask them for yourself about how they enjoyed themselves. They will be likely to be visiting her tomorrow too, and for some extended time in the days to come, as they get settled in."

She had not liked to hear any of that.

"Who is with them? Looking after them? The streets are far too dangerous for a young woman these days. I would prefer them to be here."

"George is their escort. He knows the family well, too."

"That, is no recommendation." Her own son did not rank very high, in her esteem.

"They took the carriage."

She was still dissatisfied with the too brief and even evasive replies, but would not enquire further.

When James brought her the tonic for her nerves, later that day, she asked him the same questions; getting essentially the same responses.

"And where is, Rebecca?" She had certainly missed hearing her careless laughter from time to time, or faint sounds from upstairs.

Her voice had hardened.

"I have not seen or heard anything of her for almost two days." She always liked to know where everyone was.

"Neither have I, Ma'am. However, I know she is well. Contented, eating well." He certainly knew that much.

It seemed to puzzle her, not hearing what she expected or needed to hear.

It was a constant sparring match. She wanted to know; yet didn't really want to know, and they catered to her questions without actually answering them.

"I am not sure where she is from one minute to the next, Ma'am. I haven't heard her very much for the last day or so myself. The twins will be able to tell you more."

"But the twins are not here." She was growing more impatient.

He hadn't heard her at all it seemed, and continued talking.

"But if she were ill, the twins would soon tell me of it. I would know."

She looked up at him.

"She is taking her meals upstairs then, or in her room, as she usually does? I usually hear something of her as the day goes on."

"She is certainly taking her meals, Ma'am, and is eating well, so you need not worry on that score."

She seemed puzzled and impatient with his answers. Never telling her enough, or what she really needed to know.

Not that she would have worried.

The twins had written to their father just that morning after spending the previous night being entertained by their sister. They had been excited to relate how Rebecca had become a different woman altogether now. She was boisterous and happy, having complete freedom to do what she wanted, with a music room full of those instruments she loved, and a garden that she would never tire of. She was loved by everyone around her, and had opened up like a blossom in the sunlight of a new day; which was a new life for her.

But Mrs. Deming did not need to be told of that. There would be trouble enough when she found out.

She became thoughtful and quiet.

"I think I shall take a stroll around my garden, James. She may be there, as I cannot hear her. I have not spoken to her for ages."

He knew there was no danger of her finding Rebecca there.

"She may be there, and there are some things I should speak to her about."

That would be a first, for her, as she invariably shunned all contact with Rebecca.

She picked up a shawl, and left the house by the front door.

"You have no need to accompany me, James. I know my own garden."

"Yes, Ma'am." He let her out and left the door ajar, watching as she walked part way around the house to the garden.

He would deal with her questions again when she returned, if he could not avoid her.

When she had not returned after almost an hour, he decided to find out where she had got to. It was unlikely she would have spent any more than two minutes in that garden at any time. She seemed to hate the very flowers that always gave Rebecca such happiness.

That was when he saw that the garden was empty, with no sign of Mrs. Deming; but her shawl was caught on the top of the wall and was partially over it.

He was puzzled.

She would never have climbed that wall for any reason... other than if she'd lost her mind, and she would never have done that; always so coldly calculating in everything she did over the last few years.

She had wanted to see Rebecca for a reason that would only have heaped more coals upon that young lady's head, except Rebecca was now free of all that, and was happy for the first time in many years.

When her mother discovered what had really happened, and that Rebecca was married, and gone, it would be a great surprise for her to deal with. It would be difficult to say how she would respond to that.

Anger, and a deep frustration were her usual responses to anything where Rebecca had been concerned.

He walked around the garden, seeing nothing unusual, except for Mrs. Deming not being there. He even walked outside, along the street, but of course he saw nothing there either.

Mrs. Deming was terrified of going out alone at any time.

As a last resort, he checked inside the house, covering it from top to bottom, and then repeated it; even checking that secret stairway that she supposedly knew nothing about.

Mrs. Deming had gone. But where? And why?

He told Mr. Deming of it when he returned, and they both of them checked again before it got dark, eventually seeing a single shoe, hidden under the bench, where it had fallen, almost out of sight.

It was one of the shoes that Mrs. Deming had been wearing when she had first decided to go around the garden to locate Rebecca.

She would not have climbed that wall, and she would not have gone anywhere wearing only one shoe.

"I am worried for her, James. This is not like her."

He thought for a while.

"I fear one of her own plots may have caught up with her. I ensured that I was always aware of where she went and what she was doing when she went into the city and who she met, but it can be difficult to keep track of her."

He shook his head.

"I will not turn my back on her despite her treatment of Rebecca. She needs our help now, as much as Rebecca did. She is still the woman I love and who bore our children. Why she changed, I did not understand. I still don't.

"Rebecca was once the pride of her life. She doted upon her from birth, cosseted her; did everything for her, and then this tragedy struck, with Rebecca's sight.

"My wife was never the same after that."

James knew all about it, just as Mr. Deming did.

The change had been gradual in Mrs. Deming. They had consulted every physician of merit and others too, but the outlook had always been the same.

Rebecca's sight had gone suddenly, and might return the same way, or might not. All she could do, was to be patient.

She had been very patient.

She had waited years for things to change, seeing her eldest daughter grow more and more to resemble her mother, as she had known she would, but with this dreadful affliction that would always keep her out of society and was so cruelly felt.

It was almost as though it had been a judgment upon her, her mother, and that she had failed in some way as a mother, yet she knew that she hadn't.

Mrs. Deming no longer left the house. She moped, and went through many moods; from desperation to despair, seeing the most cherished aspect of her own life; her daughter, her image, Rebecca, afflicted in the most terrible way.

Mr. Deming had dealt with it differently.

He, and the rest of the household, did not see any affliction. All they saw was a young woman who needed more love and care and whatever help they could provide, and they provided it.

As her mother abandoned her, they, the rest of her family and the entire household, grew closer to protect her.

It had been that way now, for many years as Mrs. Deming again began to .

"If I may make a suggestion, Sir."

"Of course, James. What?"

"We should let Miss Rebecca... Mrs. Hannan know, Sir. She always had a much steadier head than anyone else I ever knew, and she also picked up on so many things happening around her that I was never even aware of. The twins too, always kept their eyes open when they went out with their mother. They might know more.

"Her sense of what was happening around her, and even her god-given senses... despite that loss... were always much sharper tuned than those of anyone else. She may know something we don't know about this."

Mr. Deming did not have to think for long.

"You are right. But it is too late at this time of day, with too few hours to do anything. I'll go around and see her and the twins this evening and let her know. We shall continue doing what we can here. She may turn up any time, but I don't hold out much hope after seeing that shawl and the shoe. I fear she may have been kidnapped. That's what the signs would suggest.

"I only hope to god we find my wife before anything worse befalls her. She is here, or out there somewhere, and we need to find her."

The next morning.

Rebecca, Robert, the twins, and George were there early the following morning in Robert's carriage.

They learned that there had been no change in the circumstance from the evening before when they had first received Mr. Deming's letter.

Mrs. Deming was still missing. She could not have just walked away. It was more serious than that.

They sat in the breakfast parlor and listened, as both Mr. Deming and James filled them in, on what they had seen that previous evening in the garden, with that shawl, and the shoe, and what they suspected might have happened.

Rebecca was upset to hear about it, never wishing anything evil upon her mother, always striving to understand why her mother had turned against her as she had.

Robert stood beside her and comforted her.

Even when one's own mother did not behave toward one of her children as she should, there was never any thought of Rebecca feeling vengeful or bitter about anything. She understood the way her mother felt about her daughter's affliction, and even why she felt that way, and could only sympathize with her. She could forgive anything, and one should never wish ill upon one's own mother… or shouldn't.

When she got chance, she turned to Robert and spoke quietly to him so that others would not overhear.

"We should go into the garden, Robert. I would like to find out what I can sense about this. I think that is why Father wanted me here." That is what his letter had intimated.

She turned to her father.

"You say you found her shawl caught over the wall? Is that shawl somewhere close, Father?"

She took it from him and let Robert escort her into the garden. The others knew better than to follow them and to cause a distraction for her.

"I did not wish to say anything earlier, Robert, but the last time you and I were out here, just before that rainstorm hit us, I smelled something, faintly unpleasant, and then as quickly forgot it when the rain overwhelmed us."

And what a memory that had been; not so long ago now, bringing them so much closer together.

"That same smell is very faint on this shawl. When you and I walked in the early morning as we did those few times, I encountered that smell then, too, in the city in just one area of it."

Robert stood back and let her walk around her garden.

He would not interrupt her or break into her thoughts as she walked slowly around that area she was most familiar with, and she even sat on the bench, under the wall, for a few moments as she let her senses wander over what she could detect.

She came back to him and took his arm.

"I believe, Robert, that Mama may have fallen victim to a trap she decided to lay for me when I came out into the garden alone, except the last few times I was out here, you were always with me. I doubt any kidnapper would have chosen to take you on."

He smiled at the truth of that. One does not attempt to kidnap a young woman in presence of the man who loves her.

"I detected this same smell then; the smell of a piggery, as well as the wretched smell of a tannery. Someone was watching us and listening. They must have been very careful and quiet about it, having been warned about my sharpened senses."

She considered that.

"Oh, dear. Poor mama!" She seemed genuinely aggrieved.

She could see exactly how it could have happened.

"Mama did not know that you and I, married, so she may have assumed that when she no longer heard me in the house, that I must have been abducted.

"It must have puzzled her why no one mentioned me going missing, soon after it happened as she thought, though for the rest of the house… it hadn't happened like that. They knew exactly where I was, but she didn't. I had moved away, but she didn't know that, so she had to check.

"She must have come out to walk in the garden to see what she might find, and did not know that she was walking into the very trap she'd laid for me.

"Poor Mama! I would not wish any of that upon my worst enemy. I am told that she and I look very much alike, so it is easy to see how those people would believe that they were kidnapping me."

She knew she had to do something about it, and quickly.

"I doubt she planned anything worse for me. At least I hope she didn't. We must tell Father. He will know what to do; what enquiries to make, to change this. He still loves her, as I do."

"You are very forgiving, my love." He planted a kiss on the top of her head, feeling his affection returned.

They turned back to the house.

"We should all be that way, Robert; forgiving. She is still a good woman and was an excellent mother. I do remember that. I clearly remember her love for me, and for Father, and her growing desperation and despair when this affliction took hold of me as it did. I know she was horrified that whatever had struck me, could also get to the twins; was even afraid of them catching it from me. Maybe that is why she needed to see me removed from this house and why she kept away from me as she did.

"I am not sure what changed her, other than that fear, despite it being nothing like the influenza or smallpox, but I have always tried to understand it. I did not suffer too much in this life, as she may have feared… I had my music and my garden, and others who read to me, and saw to all of my needs. I grew to be happy, knowing that although I could not get out into society, that I still had so much to discover and to learn. It must have hurt her dreadfully to hear me playing on the harpsichord as I used to, in happier times; as she did. She taught me. Poor Mama."

Robert did not interrupt her.

"Then, I met you. My life became complete again, even without sight. I am loved. I am surrounded by nothing but love. I want for nothing. I can do almost everything for myself, which is more than anyone can say for many of those in society who have all of their senses, yet who can calmly let their lives pass them by in indolence. What a waste of their lives!”

Once back inside the house, they met with her father, and George, and she discussed what she believed she had learned. The twins did not need to be disturbed more than they were, so were left to continue what they were doing in another part of the house.

It made sense to her father, hearing Rebecca describe what she had discovered.

He kissed her.

“Thank you, my love. I now know where to look, and what to ask, though I may not ask so gently if the answers are not readily forthcoming. We should leave the twins at home. I believe we can advance this faster if we do this alone.”

The three of them left the house for the city.

Learning to trust Rebecca's senses.

They drove to an area by the river, in the midst of those particularly gruesome, and noysome, endeavors… slaughtering and tanning… along with other strange smells that Rebecca had detected on that shawl and in the garden.

However, there were several offices, of those who catered to tanning and butchering different animals and moving the results of their labors into the city, for sale, and then releasing the wastes—as little of it as possible—into the river to be flushed away on the tide, to add to the filth already in the river.

In each of them, Rebecca hung back, with Robert beside her, listening and detecting what she could in the smells which always hung about such places of business, and followed around, those who worked in them.

When her father rejoined them to go onto the next, of those few such businesses in that area of the city, she let him know what she herself had determined; that one, after the other, the smells did not exactly match, as she remembered them.

Then, it changed. Her father saw it immediately in the way Rebecca behaved. She suddenly perked up, squeezing Robert's arm to let him know, and he was ready to convey what that told him, to her father, though her father had already seen.

At that moment, the tenor of the questioning changed, making the man who had reluctantly met with them, agitated and defensive, at the sudden change in the way questions were asked, as well as the kind of questions that were asked.

"I think you should know that kidnapping, and murder are both Capital Offenses!"

Mr. Deming spoke softly as his eyes drilled into those of the man in front of him. It was as though he had struck the man directly in the face, he was so taken aback.

The sudden statement caught the man totally off guard to have that thrown at him.

He became flustered and looked around, unsure of what was happening.

"What are you talking about. Kidnapping? Murder? Nothing like that goes on around here. We slaughter animals here, and we tans the hides of them as we can, and processes them."

And what better place to get rid of someone with so much going on?

Mr. Deming's blood ran cold at the thought.

He was trembling with suppressed emotion.

Surely his wife would not have…?

"My wife, Mrs. Deming was here, in this exact office, the other day. I know she was, about a week or so ago." He would get answers and then he would decide how to respond.

Rebecca was holding onto Robert's arm in suspense.

The man behind the desk, was as if rooted to the ground in surprise as Mr. Deming continued..

"Her driver remembers her holding a handkerchief up to her nose as she came in here, into this very place."

The man in the office remembered it too. They'd never had a lady come in here before, so she had been easy to remember, but he had not been privy to the conversation that had followed that. The less he knew about what the nobs did, the better. Some of those families had some terrible dark secrets, and he wanted nothing to do with it, though the man who employed him did not mind getting involved… for a price.

Her coachman had remembered her doing exactly the same thing at each of those establishments she had visited, but this, was the one that Rebecca knew to be the one. Mr. Deming trusted her judgment above any other, in this case. The man began to stammer, not making any sense, as he gestured to somewhere behind him, as though calling out for help.

He was rescued by a more assured individual dressed more like a gentleman, who was looking them over carefully and had listened to everything that Horace and the man, had said, and who now came forward.

He spoke in an intelligent way. "Did I hear someone accuse us of kidnapping, or even murder, Horace?" He laughed easily, but it was a guarded kind of laugh.

"One needs to go down to the docks for that. Far too common in this town and too easily purchased, but not from me. We provide a more genteel kind of service, more demanding and more expensive, and it is all above board or I would not be a doing of it."

Mr. Deming looked him over. He seemed a self-assured, and confident individual. Perhaps it was not as bad as he'd feared, but he would need to know all of it.

"Kidnapping? Murder? Oh, my; such unkind things to say, and the first time I've ever heard that. I do hope you were not serious, Sir."

Horace was relieved to be taken off the hook when faced with such determination and such accusations.

The second man smiled, knowing why they were here.

"You go about your business, Horace, I'll see to this."

Horace was relieved to go.

He looked at his visitors, but began to feel uncertain about why they were here. This way of approaching him was unusual, though it had happened a few days earlier when a not so young lady had dropped in, making her own enquiries.

There was a tension about these visitors that made him uncomfortable, as well as the words that this gentleman had so casually thrown around.

Had something gone wrong with their arrangement? She had assured him that the entire family knew of it, and approved of it too. He would need to find out; but carefully.

"Mrs. Deming was here." Enough people had seen it and knew it, and he had no need to deny it, but it were still better that what they did was not widely known, or it could attract too much of the wrong kind of attention. He tried to protect his clients from other relatives who might see something to gain.

"But that was very recent, I recall. We rarely get ladies in this establishment for any reason. Servants; perhaps, sent to pick up some trotters, tripe, or tongue, or such things." He smiled, endeavoring to learn what he could without saying much.

"Umberto Foucault, at your service, Sir. Foucault, on account of my father being French, and Umberto, on account of my mother being Italian." He did not offer to shake hands.

This gentleman was not well enough relaxed for that.

"No, Sir. We don't do that… not kidnapping…and certainly not murder. Wherever did you get that impression? That is, against the law… as you say.

"However, we do move whatever anyone needs moving; furniture, trees, rocks, refuse, night soil and all. We do many different things. We even build privies as well as tear 'em down. So how may I be able to help you, Sir, along those particular lines? Or not. And might I know to whom I am speaking."

"I am Mr. Deming. Reginald Deming. Her husband." He produced his card for the man to look at.

It seemed to mean something to him.

"You were able to move… an inconvenience, for Mrs. Deming, just the other day."

Mr. Foucault was not going to admit to anything, but this man asking the questions, was not going to leave without learning something of what he did on his wife's behalf, when he should already have known it. That, was what the lady had assured him. She must have misled him. He did not seem to know what she had decided. This, was not good.

"She was in here not so very long ago, about moving a person." No point in trying to hide it.

However, all the paperwork had been completed. He'd insisted on that before anything moved forward. Now, it seemed that something had gone wrong.

Mr. Foucault was not smiling so much now.

"Perhaps if you give me more details of the individual we seem to have 'moved', and refresh my mind? Moved from where, to where?"

Mr. Deming explained, pleased to see that this man was of a more serious frame of mind now.

"Yesterday, a member of my family, my daughter… at least that was the plan… was removed from my garden. You may recall the address…"

Mr. Deming told him the house number, the street and the part of the city, even describing some features of the garden and the garden wall.

It was all well known to him.

"We found her shawl caught over the wall, and a shoe under the bench."

Mr. Foucault remembered it clearly, but had put others in charge of that. There would be no violence this time; and gentleness was called for, but sometimes the intended victims became very violent, especially if they were strong-headed males.

However, he had been assured of the gentle character of the young woman, but it would involve taking her over a wall, to avoid any slight disturbance near the house. He had been assured that she was a relatively slight, and helpless young person, so it would not be difficult, but they should not have left a shawl or a shoe behind.

"Mrs. Deming approached you over a week ago and suggested that task to you."

Mr. Deming seemed to know all about it, but why hadn't he said something to stop it if he hadn't approved?

"We have sometimes taken on a task like that, moving a 'dangerous' person out of the way for a family. Though perhaps not 'dangerous', so much as posing, a danger in some ill-defined way." To the lineage, usually, or to younger siblings.

"This one was not dangerous, and she posed no danger to anyone. There was nothing wrong with the person we are discussing, no insanity, nothing, other than in an acutely embarrassing way for my wife, but not for any other member of my family."

Mrs. Deming had not confided in him that far.

"So, why are you here, sir?"

"I wish to find that person whom you… 'relocated', as you say, and have her returned to her family. Mrs. Deming, is my wife."

Mr. Foucault had gathered that.

"She has had a change of heart and wishes to undo what she got started just a few days ago."

Mr. Foucault hesitated.

"Well, that is a rapid change of heart, indeed. If the lady herself, your wife, were to come in to suggest that same thing... or I could come…."

"That is not possible. Your intended… subject, was that young woman over there, my daughter, the one my wife suggested you should kidn… re-locate."

Mr. Foucault winced at that near slip.

Mr. Deming indicated, Rebecca.

Mr. Foucault saw the resemblance to the lady who had been in this very place not that long ago.

"But when my wife went into the garden to see if you had indeed succeeded in keeping your part of that contract, when she did not see her around the house for some little time; she, was the one who fell victim. My daughter, over there, the intended victim, was elsewhere at the time."

Mr. Foucault blanched, hearing that.

This was no laughing matter. They'd never 'taken' the wrong person before. He remembered Mrs. Deming telling him that the woman he was to 'relocate' was the only woman who was likely ever to be found in that garden, and that she also looked like a younger version of herself.

He looked again at the daughter.

This one, looked younger too. They had taken the wrong woman! Very embarrassing. It had never happened before. It must also be corrected before the word got out.

He went across to a cupboard and took out a sheaf of papers. Reading the one at the top, he looked up.

"Then that must be corrected, of course it must." He was now in a serious frame of mind.

Mr. Deming was able to relax for the first time since entering this place. He heaved a sigh of relief that his wife had not chosen a more decisive way to change what had slowly been driving her mad, over the years.

"She is on her way to Mizzenhurst Manor, down near Southport, Sir, in company of my own daughter. I always insist that a member of their own family travel with them in case they are stopped, but Mrs. Deming said that it would not be possible to find someone, so I made sure my daughter accompanied her."

It began to sound much better than Mr. Deming had at first, feared.

"They should be there by now. My daughter was to stay with her for at least a week, and see that she was settled in properly and happily. It is a very congenial and peaceful setting, that particular place, with extensive grounds and gardens. I was told, the young lady was especially fond of flowers and gardens.

"Mrs. Deming, was insistent on her being able to do that, and she paid well for it too."

Mr. Deming was happy to hear that. She was at least being well looked after, if Mr. Foucault was being honest, but his wife would be confused at what had happened to her so unexpectedly, and would be wondering what had happened to her.

"The estate is easily found; a few miles east of the city.

"They left just yesterday morning and were to break their journey at the Inn, in Stilldene, that first evening; the coaching stop, there, but they will be long gone by now.

"They usually soon adjust to the reality of what the family wants, and the family are encouraged to visit… if they can."

"It is a good family that needed some financial help over a spot of difficulty. We look after those we relocate, and in only the finest establishments, as befits their family's standing in society. Nobody else in London will help them, as we do, though I see you feared a lot worse… kidnapping… murder." He shivered at the thought. "Though even many of the finest families are not above doing that to change the lineage.

"I think you will admit, that 'relocating', is better than the alternative that some families adopt when they choose a more decisive approach to their problems. As Lord Nesbitt did the other week, with his heir, who was not right in the head, and not fit to inherit anything of his uncle's estate, and most of the family knew it. At least that was the way I understood it… rumors… you know how it is, I expect? And nothing like as it was reported in the Gazette".

"East of the city, you say?"

Mr. Deming was no longer listening closely.

"Yes, sir. East of the City."

He continued telling him of the Nesbitt rumor.

"We could have saved them from those awkward rumors had they come to see us. We could have re-located the lad, even if it was to one of the islands off the coast. I am sure that lad had no intention of climbing up to do anything to that Pigeon cote on the top of that barn, yet he did… so the accounts said, and he fell off that roof and broke his neck… so they said; poor, headstrong lad, and no one to say otherwise. Nothing could be done for him, so the article said. The family is now in mourning."

He sighed heavily.

"But his mother had a different tale to tell." He shook his head. "Very embarrassing for the family what she accused his uncle of doing to the lad! Better if he'd been moved to a safe place, and where he could do no harm, than face that. The lad could have disappeared for a while until things got sorted out with the lineage, and a new heir discovered, but… desperate times…. We could have saved the poor lad's life. I told Horace that, just the other day.

"I shall, of course, offer a full return of all monies paid, when she is returned, but I must keep the paperwork … in case."

…In case the family was playing games, and tried to blame them if worse happened.

However, no sooner had they learned where the party was headed, than they'd departed without so much as a 'thank you'.

They would find that everything was as he had described it.

He had no fear for his daughter when they came upon her and her charge.

A difficult lesson learned. A house set in order.

Mizzenhurst Manor proved not to be so easy to get to.

They checked at the Coaching stop in Stilldene, and discovered that the ones they were inquiring about, had not spent the previous night there, but had pushed on to complete their journey after their late afternoon meal, with the weather being so good.

However, the weather, and other things, conspired against Mr. Deming and his party, where it had not stopped the earlier one.

They discovered that a bridge ahead of them had washed out, hours earlier, and not only that, but one of the rims on a wheel of their carriage was working loose and would need to be repaired.

They were stuck in Stilldene for two nights as they waited for both problems to be corrected. There was no other carriage they could rent or hire to make a long detour, and had to hide their impatience and wait, able to go nowhere.

They left almost two days later.

There was no difficulty finding the estate they were aiming for, but were still not sure what lay ahead of them after that, or what would greet them.

Mrs. Deming would surely be desperate by then to see faces that she knew, and who would be there to rescue her from this unexpected fate that had befallen her.

The estate, they learned, was about 1,000 acres, and did not seem to be run down or in need of anything. It even appeared to be well-maintained. There were ground's staff, clearing dead and fallen trees after the storm that had seen them stranded, while other were replacing tiles that had blown off the roof.

They were welcomed politely, as though they were expected; a relief in itself to all of them.

Robert had kept up a running commentary of their journey to Rebecca, sensing her excitement with this new adventure, despite the reason that had made it necessary. She had never travelled so far from home before, since she had been a little girl.

Mr. Deming identified himself to the gentleman who soon came from the house to meet with them, and the introduction was reciprocated.

"Alfred Scrivenor at your service, sir. Thank you for coming so soon.It sometimes takes relatives a week, or even several, to visit. They seem reluctant, or even a little scared to visit at first, not sure what will greet them."

It sounded as though they were used to this kind of unexpected arrival. Just how many such guests, held against their wills, did they have here? And how were they being held?

Was Mrs. Deming locked away somewhere, with only her helper for company? They understood, only what Mr. Foucault had told them.

"I was led to believe that our guest, Rebecca, would be a much younger person, but I see now that I was mistaken."

He had seen Rebecca alight from the carriage on Robert's arm, and began to see the mistake that had been made, though he already knew about it. This, was the young lady that should have been here, and not her mother. The resemblance was uncanny. But this young woman was happy and was spoken for, being attended to by a protective young man. What a strangely mixed-up-circumstance this was turning out to be.

"But we soon learned otherwise when we learned her name was Suzanne, and not, Rebecca, as it should have been, though she was loath to tell us it at first; laboring as she was under such a strangely difficult burden. Nonetheless, she was made welcome, and soon settled in."

Settled in?

Mr. Deming understood none of it.His wife would never have accepted what had happened to her as easily as that, after being abducted in a way that cannot have been easily accepted or even pleasant. After that, she would have been as difficult as she could possibly be, (and he knew, firsthand, what that was like) and have agitated to have been returned 'at once' to her home. She would have kicked up a fuss that would have made them equally anxious to get rid of her. Yet it sounded as though she hadn't.

He had even half expected to cross paths with a carriage returning her to London post haste, but they hadn't.

They must have her sedated.

"We would like to see her, please."

"You will, sir, you will. When they return. You will join us for dinner, of course, and are welcome to stay the night too."

Stranger, and stranger.

"She is not here?"

"She is, but is out walking with Miss Foucault and my daughter, Diane." He laughed.

"Miss Foucault and my daughter were in school together, and made fast friends then. It seems that that friendship now embraces your relative.

"Please make yourselves at home. You may go inside if you wish if the sun out here is a little too bright." He spoke further in a friendly way

"Harriet Foucault's father is a respected businessman, and a good friend, though…" he wrinkled his nose… "his business is a little out of the ordinary, in the city. I take it, Sir, that Suzanne is your wife, and that young lady there, is your daughter?"

He seemed to understand the mistake that had been made.

Rebecca and Robert had already strolled over to the house and had gone in through open French doors at the invitation of another.

Mr. Deming nodded. This was a strange circumstance indeed.

"Are there others here? Like, my wife?"

"No, sir. There have been, in the past, but not at the present time. We help relatives to get beyond a difficult time for them. It is easily done, here." He chose not to say any more on that topic.

"Your wife has made two good friends already but is proving to be just a little bit eccentric about some things." He chuckled over some private thought that only he might be aware of.

'Eccentric', was not how Mr. Deming would describe her when things didn't go her way. She was likely to be 'difficult', or even 'impossible' and destructive.

Mr. Deming decided to be patient. He had been met by nothing but kindness so far; no evasion, and he would not respond to anything, until he knew more. None of this, sounded like his wife of a few days ago.

"The ladies decided to go out each day in the afternoon, provided the weather was good, and walk around the estate and its gardens, and, until your wife… gets used to her surroundings, she needs some escorting."

Mr. Deming did not understand. "Escorting? How? Why?"

"You will have to see that for yourself, Sir.

"Miss Foucault told me what she had learned of the actual circumstance, and what it should have been, on the long drive down. Your wife was in a strange frame of mind for that journey. Quite unexpected.

"I hope you were not planning on having her return with you immediately, and I hope you are prepared to see a very different woman than you may have been used to, even after such a short time."

Mr. Deming did not know what he was talking about.

"She is undergoing a sudden transition here, transplanted from that other environment, and it would be a shame to interrupt it before it is completed. You may stay here just as long as you wish to, to help in that process if you wish and talk through those issues."

Mr. Deming did not understand what he was talking about. 'Transition?' 'Transplanted?' 'Eccentric'?

Mrs. Deming was not eccentric in any way that he knew about, but he would remain silent and learn.

"The atmosphere here is very unlike that in the city, and is conducive…well, I'm sure you'll see.

"Do come in for some refreshments while we talk. I expect them to return shortly. We may as well relax in comfort, but I see and hear that your daughter has already discovered our music room. Her mother is also accomplished that way too, and has been teaching my daughter a few of the finer points of playing. It is easy to see where your daughter learned so well."

The sound of the Harpsichord drifted out across the lawns and seemed to draw others to the house, among them three women in a party who had appeared from the woods, arms linked, walking swiftly to the house, attracted by the music.

Mr. Deming recognised Suzanne immediately, and set out to meet them, but then held back, not understanding what he was seeing. They seemed to be playing some child's game. One of them, his wife, was barefoot and had something wrapped around her head, covering her eyes. She could not see him.

She spoke. "Do you hear that? I am sure you must. I would know that playing, anywhere. I taught her. But… it cannot be. My imagination is playing tricks on me as it always does, but I deserve it."

"We also hear it, Suzanne, so it is not in your imagination."

They could also see that they had visitors, and could guess who they were. Of course, her family would be concerned for her, no matter what she had done. She had already described her daughter and her husband and how she would need to turn her back on that other life and forget it. But that other life was not prepared to let her do that, else why was her husband here already. How had he found her so soon? Clearly, she was still well-loved, despite everything, or he would never have shown his face. Suzanne had told them about all of that difficulty of her own making that had seen her brought here, unexpectedly, instead of her daughter.

"Just another difficult burden that I must learn to bear for my foolish stupidity in turning my back upon my most cherished possessions; a family I did not appreciate. I shall bear this punishment, just as I shall bear these others. I brought it upon myself, so I must carry it. I deserve no less."

Mr. Deming walked over to her and took her hand.

"What is this, Suzanne?"

She was taken by surprise. Not expecting him to be here, almost pulling away.

"Reginald. What are you doing here? You should not be here to see me like this. You should not be here at all. How did you find me? Is that… could that possibly be Rebecca with you, playing?"

"It is indeed. With her husband." He made no move to change anything he saw about his wife. It was her choice.

Suzanne flinched as though she had been struck. She was still, and silent, as though suddenly frozen in place and time, then sobbed, overcome totally by so many emotions.

"Her husband?"

That news hit her hard.

"And I did not know. Oh, Reginald, what have I done to her, to you, to my family? How do I recover from this? How could anyone forgive me for what I did, or how I have behaved over these last few years with my own daughter whom I love, still love more than I love life itself? Least of all Rebecca. I never stopped loving her, but… the pain…seeing that change in her, after making such plans for her. It was unbearable. I do not deserve to be forgiven, and I would never ask it."

She seemed to be feeling it sorely.

"She is even married? How did I not know that? I missed all of that, and under my very nose. I was too busy fighting my own demons to see what was changing. I did not even know what was happening in my own house. When did she marry? Who? Why did I know none of it?"

Her two companions were happy just to listen to what she had to say and to Reginald's gentle responses to her.

"She was married a few days ago; one morning while you slept. That was why she was not in the house, and why you did not hear her, that time."

And was why she had gone out into the garden to check, and had been caught in the same mischief that she had plotted for her daughter.

"I never knew. I never met him. Did I?"

"No, my dear, but you came close to it, that one time; that day you caught George in the house when he did not expect you to be at home. Robert met Rebecca then, when George sent him deeper into the house to save him from you blundering into him.

"That was when he met Rebecca. They fell in love at that first moment."

A tear escaped down her cheek and she hung her head.

"Why this blindfold, my love, and where are your shoes? What game are you playing?"

"It is not a game, Reginald. I do not deserve any of you. This, shall be my punishment.

"I deserve neither sight, nor shoes. I must learn to live in Rebecca's world now, and feel what she felt, learn what she learned, and feel how difficult it was for her with a mother like me, though there is no one like me, here."

"You are being too unkind upon yourself, Suzanne. She still loves you, you know?"

"She should not. I am not loveable. I do not deserve any such love, not after what I did, turning my back on her like that when she most needed me."

She heard the music cease.

"What is her married name?"

"Rebecca Hannan, my love. She married Robert Hannan and went to live with him. The twins were with her the other day. I told you of him, but not of them being married. Her husband is here with her too."

"We would like you back, my dear."

"Why are you being so nice to me, Reginald? I do not deserve any such thing after what I did. You should have put me out from my home. Banished me. I deserved no less."

"I couldn't. I tried to understand what you were going through. You used to be a wonderful mother. It was a pleasure to watch you with her, teaching her, helping her. Then all of our dreams had to change. I saw how you were suffering under that burden, but you would not be helped. The greatest of loves, gives rise to the greatest pains. It always does. You were responding to that pain."

"But Rebecca did not deserve that."

"No, she didn't, but despite a few minor hardships, she was not harmed so much by it. We all made up for it; the entire household. We saw that she wanted for nothing. She still had us, and her garden, and we all read to her and brought her up to date on everything."

"But I was not there for her as a mother should have been. I denied her a proper mother to love her." She sighed heavily and did not move from where she stood.

"I should not meet her husband, Reginald. I imagine he could not bear to look on me, such an unnatural mother, and I do not deserve a daughter like her either. How can she bear to consider me, her mother? I am not fit to be that.

"But why are you here?"

"We came to take you back home with us."

She thought about that for a few moments.

"That is not possible. How can you consider allowing me back into your life so easily? It is too soon for that. I have too much to atone for." She braced her shoulders. "I shall stay here. I deserve no other family, yet this is not the punishment I wanted or deserve. Everything is too peaceful and kind around me here, and I have even made new friends, which I never did before. I lost friends.

"No, I should not leave here, Reginald. It is much more pleasant here than even I deserve, but at least I can think clearly without that dreadful burden of guilt that I was carrying. These are kind people and I have made two good friends already. It is too soon to leave them, and they are helping me."

He was not going to give up.

"They can visit us in London."

"I do not deserve the family I had. I do not deserve them; not George, not the twins, and especially not Rebecca. I do not deserve you."

She voiced an afterthought. "James should have poisoned me."

He laughed. "I believe he considered it from time to time, but we knew… we hoped, that you would recover."

"Mama?"

Suzanne's hand flew to her mouth and she took a step back. She was not able to speak.

Robert had explained what he had seen and heard, to Rebecca.

She repeated what her father had already said.

"You do not need to stay here, mother. We need you at home with us. We have so much to catch up on."

Suzanne dropped to her knees and slowly reached out to touch the hem of her daughter's dress.

"How can you of all people, Rebecca, think to forgive me so easily after I made your life so difficult? Look what happened to me to bring me to my senses; but it was what I had planned for you. How hurt you would have been by that experience. Thank god it did not get to that, for you. No. This, is what I deserve. I, alone."

Reginald still held her hand. "She would not have been gone for long, my dear. We would have soon found her, as we found you, had we needed to. I have no doubt of that. We had enough clues."

"Oh, Rebecca. How could I do this to you? What an unnatural mother I was, just at the time you most needed me."

"It was not so very bad, Mama. Nor is this, from what I am told, and sense. I had my garden, and my sisters who read to me, as father did. James looked after me very well. And then one day, Robert came into my life. How would I have met him on that special day, but for you? I think I should thank you for that."

She let that strange thought digest in her mother's mind.

"Of course, I shall be living with him now, but you may visit any time you wish; with your friends, and we shall visit you often, too."

The tears flowed freely down her mother's face.

"How did you know what had happened to me? I felt sure that what I did, was done without anyone knowing what I had planned. I had not intended that you would be found. I am surprised you managed to find me."

Reginald took over again, as Rebecca wiped away her mother's tears from her cheek, and kissed more of them away.

"That was Rebecca's doing, my dear."

Suzanne was feeling it especially cruelly, now; being helped, forgiven, knowing that she was loved.

"James found your shawl and a shoe in the garden, but Rebecca told us what had happened to you when she followed the direction that her senses led her.

"We located Mr. Foucault, and soon found out what had happened. He told us exactly where you were, so that we could correct that mistake, but we were held up for two days."

"You should have left me here. It was fitting that I was caught up in a trap of my own making. Thank god it was me, and not Rebecca. It was a needed wake-up call to me.

"I honestly thought that the end of the world had come when that blanket was put over my head and I was lifted over that wall as though I weighed nothing.

"The world ended then, for me. The end of that world I had just left. I had even planned on that happening to my own daughter; my own flesh and blood." She shook her head and groaned, "but this will never be penance enough for that. This is too kind a place for me.

"Then I realised that this, what was happening to me and not to Rebecca, was god's message to me, a judgement visited upon me, so I kept quiet and let it go where it would, I deserved no less."

Rebecca took her other hand and dropped to her knees with her mother.

"Miss Foucault… Harriet, and Diane, my companions now, were all kindness, so I said nothing for a while, then I had to tell them. They wanted to correct it; return me to London, but I dissuaded them. I told them about me, and what I had done, so they resolved to leave it with me.

"They are my guides until I learn this life. Whatever happened to me, I deserved it, but I wound up in heaven, which is what this place is, and not the hell I deserved, so I had to punish myself. I decided that I should learn what my daughter, you, my love, had learned; felt… but I told you that.

"It is not so very bad. I am learning my way about, and I have my music. I am also learning to 'see' other things in a different way. I have only stubbed my toes a few times, stepped on thorns twice, walked into furniture and trees, but I have not yet been stung.I will soon learn my way about.

"I have taken in interest in music again, and have begun to teach Diane, though she is already accomplished. My ear for music is improving. You were right. When one loses one sense, the others become sharper.

She reached out to Rebecca.

"I have no right to ask. But do you think you can ever forgive me, my love?"

She felt Rebecca loosen her blindfold and take it off.

"You do not need this, Mama. You do not need to stay here, pleasant as I know it must be.

"We need you at home. We need you back in our lives now."

www.ingramcontent.com/pod-product-compliance
Lightning Source LLC
Chambersburg PA
CBHW061514120726
48001CB00004B/1321